A MAGNIFICENT EPOCH OF WORLD WAR II

What occurred off Midway Island on June 4, 1942, became the finest single chapter in American naval history. No other hour shines more brightly in the annals of war. The names of the individual pilots faded long ago, but their deeds, and their sacrifices, live on.

After Midway, one thing was certain: the Japanese naval war machine was suddenly on the defensive. Midway stopped its advance. Forever. From Midway on, the offensive in the Pacific clearly belonged to the U.S. armed forces.

Here, now, is the entire astounding story.

Avon Books are available at special quantity discounts
for bulk purchases for sales promotions, premiums,
fund raising or educational use. Special books, or
book excerpts, can also be created to fit specific needs.

For details write or telephone the office of the Direc-
tor of Special Markets, Avon Books, 959 8th Avenue,
New York, New York 10019, 212-262-3361.

THE BATTLE OFF MIDWAY ISLAND

THEODORE TAYLOR

**First in a series of
The Great Sea Battles of World War II**

Illustrated by Andrew Glass

AN AVON  FLARE BOOK

THE BATTLE OFF MIDWAY ISLAND is an original publication of Avon Books. This work has never before appeared in book form.

Library of Congress Cataloging in Publication Data

Taylor, Theodore, 1922-
  The battle off Midway Island.

  (The Great Battles of World War II ; 1) (An Avon flare book)
  Bibliography: p. 135
  Includes index.
  Summary: An account of the June, 1942, air battle between American and Japanese forces which proved a decisive defeat for the Japanese and the turning point of the war in the Pacific.

  1. Midway, Battle of, 1942—Juvenile literature.

[1. Midway, Battle of 1942. 2. World War, 1939-1945—Naval operations, American] I. Glass, Andrew, ill.
II. Title.   III. Series: Taylor, Theodore, 1922-
Great sea battles of World War II ; 1.
D774.M5T38   940.54'26   80-69946
ISBN 0-380-78790-3   AACR2

AVON BOOKS
A division of
The Hearst Corporation
959 Eighth Avenue
New York, New York 10019

Copyright © 1981 by Theodore Taylor
Published by arrangement with the author
Library of Congress Catalog Card Number: 80-69946
ISBN: 0-380-78790-3

First Flare Printing, October, 1981

FLARE trademark application is pending before the U.S. Patent and Trademark Office.

Printed in the U.S.A.

WFH 10 9 8 7 6 5 4 3 2

For
CHRISTOPHER ROBIN,
who suggested this book.

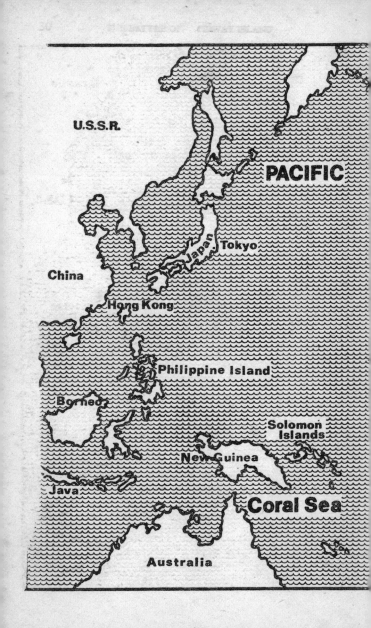

U.S.S.R.

PACIFIC

China

Japan

Tokyo

Hong Kong

Philippine Island

Borneo

Solomon
Islands

Java

New Guinea

Coral Sea

Australia

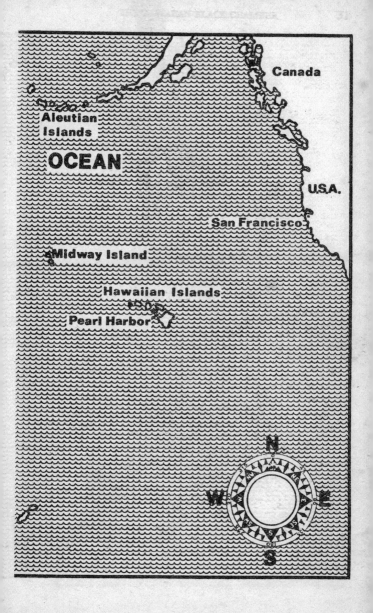

Canada

Aleutian
Islands

OCEAN

U.S.A.

San Francisco

Midway Island

Hawaiian Islands

Pearl Harbor

N

W   E

S

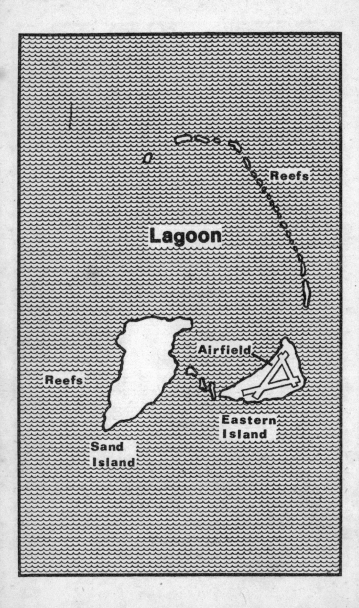

Table of Contents

Gooneyland: A Preface

Midway Island, 1,136 miles west-northwest of Honolulu in the vast Central Pacific, was anything but exotic in 1859 when Captain Brooks of the American bark *Gambia* took possession of it for the United States. There was no resistance from anyone at all. Though part of the beautiful Hawaiian chain of islands, the tiny, grubby, low-lying atoll had no tropical splendor, not even a lone palm tree, and no other nation had ever shown a specific interest in acquiring it. Apparently, the early Polynesian adventurers had paddled on by and ignored it.

For years, the only inhabitants who truly seemed to appreciate Midway with its lovely blue-green lagoon in the center were noisy families of sea birds—shearwaters, wild canaries, terns, gannets, rails and the funny, awkward Laysan albatross also called the "gooney." The birds had probably nested there for centuries, occasionally attracting Japanese feather collectors.

The atoll seemed to have a special appeal to the goonies, perhaps because it was a safe place to lay eggs. Thousands of them made up the loud, clacking majority of this small island midway from California to Japan, constantly crash-landing in the lagoon and waddling on the white sand beaches.

Yet the atoll did have some intriguing history due to sailing ships stopping there in the nineteenth century,

11

for one reason or another. Murder had been committed on its shores. It was also the site of several shipwrecks, including the British *Wandering Minstrel* in 1887, which was the inspiration for Robert Lewis Stevenson's *The Wrecker*.

The coral reef atoll is scarcely six miles in width, was formed by two islets—shoe-shaped Sand and triangular Eastern, neither more than two miles long. Sailors were never fond of Midway because it lacked Polynesian girls, pretty or not. And the only real value of Midway for a long time was its use as a junction for the Honolulu-Guam-Manila communications cable, which was owned by the Pacific Commercial Cable Company.

The United States Navy had been the unwilling proprietor of the island since 1903, establishing a lighthouse and stationing a small, temporary garrison of Marines to discourage further feather collecting by the Japanese. The goonies were safe, but the Marines were in danger of going insane from the inactivity.

Though the cable workers planted trees, seeded lawns, and imported chickens and cattle from Honolulu, the island mostly dozed under the strong sun and dazzling blue skies until 1935 when Pan American Airways chose Sand Island as a stop for its famed Clippers, the big flying boats that crossed the Pacific.

Suddenly, there was a seaplane ramp, a small hotel and maintenance sheds. The outside world began to discover the islets of Sand and Eastern. Navy seaplanes now flew into Midway on training exercises. The island was no longer a sleepy, unwanted "gooneyland." In fact, the Navy had plans for Midway. In Washington officers eyed the atoll's position on the nautical charts and decided it might make an ideal defensive base should Japan continue its aggressive attitudes in the Pacific and Far East.

Japan had been warlike for several years, sending troops into the Chinese province of Manchuria in 1931 for the sole purpose of expanding their empire. China was attacked again in 1937 by Japanese troops and aircraft. The great cities of Peking and Shanghai fell to Japanese troops that year.

But these "Asian" wars, which often seemed so remote, were soon overshadowed by Germany's aggressions in Europe. The headlines were taken over by Germany's mad dictator, Adolf Hitler, who sent tanks into Austria in 1938, then captured Czechoslovakia in a bloodless coup later in the year. Hitler's armies then invaded Poland the next year, a startling move answered quickly by a declaration of war from Great Britain and France. Gunfire began to echo over all of Europe.

None of these earthshaking events disturbed Midway in the slightest. They were occurring thousands of miles from the mid-Pacific and seemed almost unreal. The cable workers and Marines continued to fish and swim, and the few Pan Am workers tended the weekly Clipper flights. All was peaceful on Sand and Eastern atolls.

However, events *were* occurring much closer to Midway. At army headquarters on Miyakezaka Hill in Tokyo, a small number of hot-headed but influential Japanese officers were urging military action in the Pacific. Being of the *samurai* spirit, the ancient Japanese warrior code, they actively sought war. It appeared that these officers would like to send Japan to war against any nation for any reason. Majors and colonels finally influenced the older, more moderate officers.

When not engaged in assaulting China, the militarists were busily influencing Japanese writers, commentators and politicians to restore the old dream of *Hakko-Ichiu*—". . . bringing the eight corners of the world under one roof," Japan's roof! This dream put on a modern dress called "The Greater East Asia Co-Prosperity Sphere," with Japan leading a vast industrial empire composed of China, Burma, Malaya, Indochina, the Philippine Islands and the oil-rich

Netherlands East Indies. If she succeeded, all of Asia would be dominated by Japan, regardless of the feelings and desires of such individual nations as Burma and the Philippines.

But behind the *samurai* spirit were other considerations of even more importance—money and trade. Japan needed raw materials and population resources to compete with the Western countries. This nation, confined to relatively small islands with too few natural resources, yearned to be equal in the markets of the modern world.

In 1940, while Japan invaded the defenseless Netherlands East Indies to capture natural resources, Germany marched on Norway, Denmark, Holland, Belgium, Luxembourg and France. In these same anguished months of 1940, Japan signed military pacts with Hitler and Italy's pompous dictator, Benito Mussolini, promising not to interfere in Europe if they would give Japan a free hand in the Far East.

During this time, the United States had remained anxiously on the sidelines, though avoiding hostilities, aiding Great Britain with war supplies and antagonizing Japan with commerce sanctions. Assets of Japan in America were "frozen" and oil shipments were restricted.

Japan's militarists soon decided for war, but the dream of *Hakko-Ichiu* was to shatter off the little island called Midway.

1. The Sentry Island

By late summer 1941, Midway, code named BALSA, has become the busy home of a U.S. Naval Air Station, a base for Catalina-type PBY flying boats, a twin-engined amphibious patrol aircraft. Each day, they take off from the blue lagoon and range far out over the Pacific looking for potential enemy activity. Military planners are more worried than ever about Japan and her Central Pacific intentions, therefore Midway takes on an importance never imagined by Captain Brooks of the *Gambia*.

Construction is started on 5,300-foot airstrips on Eastern Island for land-based patrol planes. Hangars, fuel tanks, and other facilities begin to take shape as civilian workers swarm over the islands. A battalion of Marines disembarks to set up shore batteries and other defenses. Midway is now a full-fledged "sentry" of the Hawaiian group—the outermost sentry.

On the morning of December 7, 1941, it becomes something more than a sentry. At approximately 6 A.M., in Midway, 8 A.M. in Honolulu, the island hears startling news from a distant neighbor: *Air raid!* The Japanese are attacking the United States naval base at Pearl Harbor, on the Hawaiian island of Oahu.

Throughout the long, nervous day, Midway awaits its own punishment from the Japanese Imperial Navy. Guns have been manned since dawn; aircraft are in readiness for either combat or escape from being caught on the ground during raids. The lumbering PBY Catalinas are air-borne for long-range searches.

Signs that the waiting will soon be over come at about 6:45 P.M. when a Marine lookout reports a flashing light on the horizon, obviously from signaling ships. Darkness has enclosed Sand and Eastern, but shelter is denied the atolls. A bright moon is shining as the suspense ends when the Japanese destroyers *Ushio* and *Sazanami* open fire. Salvos come whistling in.

Midway's still-meager defense batteries return the shelling, which lasts twenty-three minutes. Then the *Ushio* and *Sazanami* depart. Damage to the island installations is not serious, and casualties from shrapnel are light.

The brief attack on Midway is clearly of a nuisance nature. It serves as a warning that the Japanese will be back, and not to collect feathers. In fact, a full strike, using the carrier planes from the Pearl Harbor raid, had been planned. However, bad weather caused the returning flattops to forego Midway. Instead, two of the carriers, the *Soryu* and *Hiryu,* are sent to attack Wake Island, a larger atoll 1,182 miles to the west of Midway.

Sooner or later, the Japanese are certain to return and the recent efforts to bolster Midway's defenses are quadrupled. On December 17, seventeen old dive bombers, Chance-Vought Vindicators, fly in from Pearl Harbor, led by a pokey PBY. Not one of the single-engine aircraft is lost on the long flight over water, almost a miracle despite their recently fitted extra gas tanks. Then, on Christmas Day, the island receives a most welcome and morale-building gift— fourteen fighter aircraft, ancient Brewster Buffalos, which pilots call "Flying Coffins." Matching the Vindicator and the Buffalo against the fast, highly maneuverable Japanese Zero is like pitting a fly against a wasp. To nonaviators, however, they are a comforting sight on the sun-baked airstrips of Eastern. The pilots still look at them and shudder. Flying coffins.

The year ends with continued preparation on Midway as it is now known that Wake Island is in Japanese hands despite a heroic defense. Guam fell on December 10.

Midway is very much alone out here more than a thousand miles from Hawaii. Her cable to Guam and Manila is still open but now useless. Now and then, someone sends some curses over that portion of the cable for Japanese reading. The Hawaii section is now very active and priceless because messages can be sent to Pearl Harbor without any chance of the Japanese overhearing them.

2. Victory Fever

One hundred and twelve days have passed since Japan's carrier aircraft bombed "Battleship Row" in Pearl Harbor to begin the Pacific war, and in Tokyo, the bustling Japanese capital, already there is talk of a quick and total victory. In fact, "victory fever," a sometimes dangerous malady of war, is in the spring air throughout the countryside.

Such loose talk greatly disturbs at least one prominent Japanese, the famed Admiral Isoroku Yamamoto, commander in chief of the Imperial Navy's Combined Fleet. He is the courteous, soft-spoken officer who ordered the bombing of Pearl Harbor. Victory over the stubborn United States will not come easily, if at all, Yamamoto has long maintained.

It is Monday, March 29, 1942, and the immaculate admiral—a compact, athletic man with sharp eyes—is aboard his flagship, *Yamato,* the world's largest battleship, moored to fat red buoys at Hashirajima anchorage in the quiet Inland Sea not far from the city of Hiroshima. More than fifty other ships of the Combined Fleet, all studded with guns and some with torpedo tubes, surround the *Yamato,* where business at the sea ladder is brisk. Officers come and go in a steady stream to this huge floating headquarters, some paying calls on the commander in chief himself.

In a working space on the battleship not far from Yamamoto's living quarters and office, members of the admiral's large War Plans Staff are putting together strategy for the complete destruction of the major United States sea forces in the Pacific.

Once the American ships are sunk, especially the aircraft carriers, Yamamoto's planners project that the Japanese armies may not have to invade and occupy the Hawaiian Islands, nor attack the West Coast of the United States. It is firmly believed by some experts, both military and political, that America will plead for peace soon after her ships are destroyed. After all, the Americans will have lost their ability to defend themselves in the Pacific, they say. Experts also point out that the "Yankees" haven't shown much ability in sea warfare, nor have they shown any real desire to fight, aside from some hit and run raids against Japanese-held islands by the U.S. carriers *Enterprise, Yorktown* and *Lexington,* which caused little damage.

The new plan is top secret, of course. The site of the proposed island invasion in the Central Pacific, which will probably force the reluctant Americans to send their main fleet into battle, is known only as *AF,* its code designation. Early June 1942 is the time chosen by Admiral Yamamoto to deliver this final, devastating blow to the U.S. Pacific Fleet, which is already battered by the bombing of Pearl Harbor. The moon will be full then, ideal for night battles should they occur. Yamamoto prefers to fight at night, as do most of his admirals, using the huge guns of the battleships and the darting, slashing torpedo attacks of the destroyers.

Spurred on by the militant army officers on Miyakezaka Hill, Japan is succeeding in the war beyond her most hopeful dreams. Most of the military and political leaders consider the Pearl Harbor raid a huge success even though none of the American aircraft carriers were in port that day, because a number of battleships and other fighting vessels were sunk or damaged.

Perhaps the largest achievement has been Japan's pride in thinking that their Navy dared to make that attack. The current "victory fever" is part of that pride.

There have been many victories since December 7. Great Britain's Asian Fleet was destroyed by the Japanese Navy led by carrier aircraft. Wake Island, Guam and Hong Kong have been captured. Thailand, North Borneo, Singapore, Northern New Guinea, New Britain, New Ireland and the entire Netherlands East Indies are all in Japanese hands. Many smaller, more remote places have been captured.

The Philippine Islands, American possessions, are soon to fall—a bitter, humiliating blow to the United States, and strategically, a disaster. There are many American troops in the Philippines as well as a major naval base. Military commanders have admitted that they cannot hold the Philippines.

By March, as the four main islands of Japan are turning green after an exciting, triumphant winter, Japan has already conquered all the territories she will need for years to come. Retaining them is largely a matter of defeating America, a task that does not seem impossible at all. *Hakko-Ichiu* can come later.

Having won the territories by hard combat, now Japan's job is to establish a *home defense line* running from the Kurile Islands off the Russian coast to Wake Island in the central Pacific, then around the southern and western edges of the Malay Barrier to the Burmese-Indian border. It is a vast semicircle behind which Japan plans to stay and, for the moment, vigorously guard her newly acquired holdings. But standing in the way of establishing this defense line is what is left of the U.S. Pacific Fleet and a blue-eyed Texan named Chester Nimitz, recently appointed Commander in Chief, Pacific, or CINCPAC, with headquarters at Pearl Harbor.

Admiral Nimitz and Admiral Yamamoto both know that whoever controls a sea usually also controls the land masses surrounded by that sea. They are also well aware that military equipment and supplies must move over the sea lanes to support their armies on land.

Nimitz plans eventually to deny those sea lanes to Admiral Yamamoto and take back control of the Pacific Ocean.

True, Nimitz hasn't shown much in the way of offense thus far, other than those token carrier raids against Japanese installations in the Marshall and Gilbert Islands; a raid against Wake, and another in the New Guinea area. There have been no decisive actions, however, nothing to cause the Japanese Navy any concern. CINCPAC needs more time.

Nimitz can also be thankful that there isn't much in the way of "victory fever" in the United States. Shipyards and aircraft factories back home are working around the clock. Ammunition, guns and tanks are starting to pour out of American plants. Millions of men are in training for military service. Everyone seems too busy to waste time talking about victory.

And while Pearl Harbor at first appeared to be a paralyzing defeat for America, there are some doubts about that now. The raid united the American people, enraging them. Japan will find that rage and determination are also weapons of war.

3. Isoruku Yamamoto

Wounded at the Battle of Tsushima during Admiral Togo's great victory over the Russians in 1908, Admiral Yamamoto has two fingers missing from his left hand, which is no handicap when playing all night poker or bridge. He is expert at both and was the Japanese Navy's champion at *Go* and *Shogi*, games similar to checkers and chess. The games indicate his thinking and spirit of competition.

Socially, he is a charming man, though he doesn't like cocktail parties and such. He drinks nothing stronger than tea. Although he is a dignified man, he'll stand on his head or do a wild peasant dance when the occasion calls for it. Married and the father of four children, Yamamoto doesn't see much of his family. He spends most of his free time with a pretty geisha girl named Kikuji, which means "Chrysanthemum Way." Geishas are women who entertain. Kikuji sings to the admiral, or plays her *samisen*, a Japanese stringed instrument, for him. She often dines and plays cards with him. Admiral Chester Nimitz, who was born in Fredericksburg, Texas, in 1885, is a family man, beloved by the men who serve under him, and seems rather dull in contrast.

Little is known in America about Isoroku Yamamoto. Hated as the Pearl Harbor raider, it is rumored that he constantly boasts that he will "dictate peace in the White House." In fact, he made no such statement.

At the Pearl Harbor victory party, Yamamoto seemed to be the least merry of all the high-ranking officers there. He called the raid a "small success," while others bragged about it. Yamamoto had no initial desire to go to war against the United States. He was outspoken in his opposition to the army "hot heads" who favored attacks on America and Great Britain. This strong opposition endangered his life at one point, and he was sent to sea to avoid assassination.

Unlike most of the Japanese military men, he knows a great deal about America. He studied at Harvard University and served for a while as a Japanese naval attaché in Washington. He'd also traveled all over the country by train and bus, and personally witnessed the industrial might of such cities as Pittsburgh and Detroit. Japan could never match that strength, he'd said, continuing to argue against war until the fall of 1941. When his superiors decided to fight, however, Yamamoto stopped his opposition and devoted himself wholeheartedly to his orders—to fight and win.

In the months before the attack on Hawaii, Yamamoto told Japan's former premier, Prince Fumimaro Konoye, "I can run wild for the first six months or a year, but I have utterly no confidence for the second or third years of fighting." He has not changed his mind and six months of the war have almost passed. Thus, there is great urgency in preparing this plan to attack and then invade *AF,* in the Central Pacific, baiting the U.S. fleet to make it come out and fight so that they can sink it.

But *AF* is far away from the Japanese home islands and a number of naval planners, particularly those of the Naval General Staff, the supreme headquarters staff in Tokyo, think that other objectives are more important at this time. A number of high-ranking admirals agree. In addition, the generals who will have to supply the invasion troops and then defend the island, don't care for the idea. The long distance to

AF bothers them. Many Japanese military men, both army and navy, tend to believe in defense more than offense: *"Let the enemy come to us. We will then annihiliate him."*

Aboard the battleship this March day are Yamamoto and his staff, the "operating men," the fighting men involved in carrying out the overall strategy of Tokyo's high command. They favor the Central Pacific attack on *AF* for a single reason: the opportunity to throw their superior carrier forces against the U.S. Navy's supposedly inferior flattops. Once the U.S. carriers are destroyed, Yamamoto is free to go where he pleases in the Pacific. The actual invasion of the island is secondary in his mind.

Yamamoto has more carriers—ten "first class" to Americas' seven—with better aircraft and pilots with more experience than those manning the U.S. planes. All of Yamamoto's carriers are in the Pacific while the U.S. must keep several of hers in the Atlantic to fight a two-ocean war. The odds do favor a tremendous victory for Japan, and Yamamoto remains the gambler whether it's with cards and dice, or ships and men.

In early April, Yamamoto's planning officer departs from the Hashirajima anchorage and goes to Tokyo to present the *AF* invasion plan, now designated Operation MI for Midway, to the Naval General Staff at headquarters. Yamamoto remains on his flagship, anticipating resistance from Tokyo. He purposely sends a comparatively low-ranking officer.

The Naval General Staff had been against the Pearl Harbor attack and now opposes Operation MI even more. They term the plan "foolhardy and unnecessary." The wisdom of occupying an island so close to Hawaii is questioned. Once occupied, can it be defended? Furthermore, is there any guarantee that the U.S. fleet will come out and fight?

With rejection looming, Yamamoto sends a stern

message to Tokyo: *"The success of our entire strategy in the Pacific will be determined by whether we succeed in destroying the United States fleet, particularly its carrier task forces. . . ."* In Yamamoto's opinion, those U.S. carriers have the capability of stopping the Japanese war machine.

The disagreement continues throughout April. Then late in the morning of April 18, war advocate General Hideki Tojo, who had succeeded the weak and ineffective Prince Konoye as prime minister, is aloft in an aircraft on an inspection tour. Suddenly the sky near him is violated by a twin-engined, brown aircraft with a white star on its side. It is definitely military, but certainly not Japanese.

Tojo's plane dodges the hurtling bomber and a gasp is heard. *American!*

It is a B-25 launched from the U.S. carrier *Hornet,* operating with the *U.S.S. Enterprise* in a task force commanded by Vice-Admiral William "Bull" Halsey, now fleeing eastward after having accomplished the launching. The Army Air Force bombers are being led to Tokyo and other cities by Colonel James Doolittle. This daring thrust by an American carrier force to the very doorway of Japan is a one-time operation designed to bolster public morale in the United States and shake the confidence of the Japanese people. It succeeds in doing both.

Though the damage to Tokyo, Yokohama, Nagoya, Kobe and other large cities is light, the psychological damage is heavy. The Japanese people cannot believe it. Their islands have always been "sacred." Fighting has always been far away from their homeland. They've been told that the American fleet was sunk on December 7 at Pearl Harbor, and that the American people have no will to fight.

Japan does not have radar as yet to alert them against air attack, and the bombers come and go before any defense can be made. The raid is a com-

plete surprise; Yamamoto takes it as a personal in-
sult, a blow to his considerable pride. He is obsessed
with protecting Tokyo, home of the emperor. Each
day at Hashirajima he asks, "What is the weather in
Tokyo?" If it is cloudy, he relaxes because bombing
is more difficult in cloudy weather. Yamamoto feels
personally responsible because the American carriers
escape without retaliation. He secludes himself in his
Yamato cabin for the rest of the day, refusing to see
all visitors.

But whatever arguments there were against *Operation MI,* the Combined Fleet campaign for the Central Pacific invasions, are abandoned by midafternoon.
Unless the American carriers, which have eluded
any contact with Japanese forces so far, are destroyed
once and for all, there will be more raids on Tokyo
and possibly defeat in Pacific as Yamamoto has predicted.

In the days just after the Hawaii raid, the brilliant
Commander Minoru Genda, who had divised the
plans for that raid, said that Midway Island should
definitely be invaded and occupied as Japan's front
outpost in that long line of defense stretching from
Russia to the Indian Ocean. More importantly, he
also said that the U.S. carriers should be lured out
and forced into a final battle. *Operation MI* reflects
Genda's earlier thinking, as well as Yamamoto's,
though the larger and smaller outlines of it have been
contributed by naval planner Captain Kameto
Kurashima, a strange and mystical man with a shaven
head, who spends hours in his darkened cabin in the
Yamato deep in meditation. He is thought by some
to be insane.

On or about May 5, *MI Plan* is presented to the
Chief of the Naval General Staff, Yamamoto's superior, Admiral Osami Nagano. He promptly approves
it, and then acting in the name of the emperor, issues Imperial General Headquarters Navy Order No.
18: ". . . to carry out occupation of *AF* and key

points in the west Aleutians in cooperation with the Army."

Certain of its conquest, the Japanese have already given Midway an appropriate new name, "Glorious Month of June."

4. The Hawaiian Black Chamber

"Hypo" is the code name for the Combat Intelligence Unit of the fourteenth Naval District, Pearl Harbor, and Hypo's intercept station at Wailupe, also on Oahu, is busy around the clock listening to coded Japanese naval messages. There is a similar unit in Washington, D.C., code-named "Negat," and another in Melbourne, Australia, code-named "Belconnen."

Hypo is also known within a very limited Navy circle as the "Black Chamber," a term that dates back to the 1700s. Originally it referred to the room where the diplomatic mail of other nations was secretly read by spies. Black Chamber is a very fitting name for the intelligence unit. Sunlight never penetrates the work space in the long, narrow, windowless basement of the District Administration Building in the Navy Yard. Steel-barred doors are at the top and bottom of the steps. Armed guards closely check the identification of all visitors, including Admiral Nimitz. Hypo's many secrets would benefit any enemy agent.

Hypo, Negat and Belconnen deal with Japan's top naval code, JN-25, which was broken by American intelligence in 1940. The units cannot hope to read and analyze all the dot-dash messages sent in JN-25, sometimes a thousand a day. However the intelligence officers and cryptoanalysts, the experts at making sense of jumbles of letters, or figures, manage to piece together much valuable information. For example; a certain enemy ship will send a message to a certain enemy command in code, and the station at Wailupe will copy it. Hypo then decodes it, noting the relation between the two and analyzing what the message probably means. The command may give orders to several other ships and another link is thereby established. The coded name of the destination then becomes known and all three ships are eventually placed at that one spot.

The solving of intricate puzzles every day is painstaking, brain-wracking work. It requires rare skills, imagination and great patience. The whole course of the war can turn on it; the fate of Midway Island does turn on the work of Hypo, Negat and Belconnen.

Japan is not aware that JN-25 has been broken; that Nimitz and his officers are constantly piecing together intelligence information. Both Morse-coded and voice transmissions are intercepted whenever possible. Nevertheless, Japan's land and sea communicators attempt to conceal the identity of their transmitters by changing the call letters frequently. But skilled listeners can usually track them down by the sound of the operator's key or "fist." Every operator, both friendly or enemy, has a distinctive touch.

In charge of Hypo is Lieutenant Commander Joseph J. Rochefort. A veteran code breaker who helped break JN-25, he is given to wearing bedroom slippers and other forms of casual dress on the job. Hypo is not a "spit and polish" outfit. Rochefort has been a radio detective since the 1920s. A tall and thin thinker who usually appears harried, sometimes ankle-deep in paper in the Black Chamber, Rochefort sends important work each day to his counterpart, Lieutenant Commander Edwin Layton, intelligence officer for Admiral Nimitz.

Layton briefs Nimitz daily on what the enemy is doing, or is likely to do, based on the monitored Japanese messages. Before taking command in the Pacfic, Nimitz had no great faith in the Black Chamber or in "radio intelligence." He still questions the accuracy of the messages, but Layton and Rochefort are slowly changing CINCPAC's mind.

For sometime, Allied war planners have surmised that Japan would eventually attempt to land troops at Port Moresby on the Papuan Peninsula of New Guinea as part of their larger effort to isolate Australia. Japan has already occupied many islands in that area, and to a degree controls the entrance to the Bismarck Sea, the body of water off New Guinea and New Britain.

The Japanese now plan to control the entire Coral Sea, which borders on Australia. With mastery of the Coral Sea, they can freely harass Australia. Vice Admiral Chuichi Nagumo, the Pearl Harbor raid commander, has already dropped bombs on the port city of Darwin. If allowed, he'll return again and again with his swift carriers. In addition to containing Australia, the Coral Sea invasion will reap many other rewards for the Japanese.

Looking at a map, the U.S. war planners at Pearl Harbor can see that the islands on the edge of the Coral Sea step down from New Britain in a slow curve—the Solomons, the Santa Cruz Islands, the New Hebrides and finally, New Caledonia. New Caledonia alone is a prize with its rich mineral resources of chrome, nickel, lead, zinc and high-grade iron ore. Japanese capture of these islands will not only help solidify their Coral Sea control and expansion in the South Pacific, but will feed their hungry war machine as well.

Throughout April, the Hypo, Negat and Belconnen monitors overhear increased radio traffic from the Imperial Fleet operators, much of it concerned with the Coral Sea-Port Moresby assault, code named *MO*. They now know the "when and where" of this latest invasion. Rochefort and Layton have told Nimitz that the Japanese may have as many as five carriers participating in *MO*. The carriers' job, as usual for seaborne invasions, will be to protect the transports and support vessels that will sail into the Coral Sea, standing between them and any forces that Admiral Nimitz might send into action.

Nimitz has also been informed that it is unlikely that Admiral Nagumo, currently Japan's top air admiral, will be present with his *Akagi*. Nagumo has been on a rampage one-third the way around the world. Beginning in December off Hawaii and in the Pearl Harbor raid, he's operated from Australia to the East Indies, then Java, Sumatra and Singapore, and most recently around Ceylon in the Indian Ocean. Without losing a single ship of his own, Nagumo has sunk five Allied battleships, an aircraft carrier (the small British *Hermes*), two cruisers and seven destroyers. He has damaged more than a hundred other ships. His planes have attacked and sunk over 200,-000 tons of Allied merchant shipping.

Nimitz is impressed with the skills and capabilities of the enemy carriers, but regrets that Nagumo might not be around for *MO*. He nonetheless thinks that it is high time to confront the Imperial Navy in a carrier battle and views the Coral Sea as a possible initial test of strength. He is determined to put all of his available sea power on the line. Unfortunately, for the moment CINCPAC has only one carrier in that area, the *Yorktown*. In a few days, however, he'll add the *Lexington*.

5. The Carriers

For the first time in modern American naval operations, battleships do not have a role in a major sea offensive. The ones that Nimitz could use in the Coral Sea are older and slower than the carriers, therefore they can't keep pace as a part of the defensive screen. Also, they require huge amounts of fuel, and there are no maintenance bases for them in the forward areas.

The carriers will be escorted by faster destroyers and cruisers, guarding against a variety of attacks from the air, the surface of the sea and below it. The destroyers are assigned the antisubmarine chores in addition to antiaircraft fire and rescuing downed pilots. The cruisers will be present to duel with long-range ship guns should enemy surface units close in on the carriers. They will also join in the antiaircraft barrages on the approach of enemy aircraft, the greatest single danger to the flattops.

The carriers, cruisers and destroyers operate in task groups or task forces. The task group may be a single carrier with its escorts, or several carriers with their escorting vessels. One or more rear admirals will command the groups. A task force may contain one or more groups and is commanded by a senior rear admiral or a vice admiral such as "Bull" Halsey. The composition of a group or force depends on the particular mission, and it is possible for only one carrier to be designated as a force.

For Coral Sea, U.S. Task Force 17 will be commanded by Rear Admiral Frank Jack Fletcher, an Iowan, flying his flag from the carrier *U.S.S. Yorktown*. Though not a "brown shoe" or aviation admiral, Fletcher is a calm and calculating man most intent on carrying out Nimitz's orders to stop the invasion of Port Moresby. In addition to the *Yorktown*, Fletcher has the *U.S.S. Lexington*, the beloved "Lady Lex." The two carriers compose Task Group 17.5, which is commanded by Rear Admiral Aubrey Fitch, a pilot and, therefore, a "brown shoe" admiral. Fletcher, like all surface admirals, wears black shoes. Fletcher is senior, automatically the force or over-all commander.

The aircraft carrier, just coming of age in 1942, exists for its flight deck just as the battleship lived for its main batteries, the heavy guns capable of hurling more than a ton of steel for several miles. Each heavy carrier may be a bit different in design, but each possesses the same facilities for flying and controlling of aircraft. The flight decks are around 800-feet in length and 115-feet in width or "beam." They operate around eighty aircraft—fighters, bombers and torpedo planes. A carrier's antiaircraft batteries are solely for defense.

The "island" on the starboard side of the flight deck is the nerve center of the ship, housing the ship's navigating bridge, Primary Fly Control (for direction of takeoffs and landings), Air Plot (for pilot navigational information), Communications, Aerological (weather information) and the pilot house, which contains the ship's navigational bridge. Also in the island is a duplicate flag officer's plotting room and bridge. A task force or group commander, such as Admiral Fletcher, is usually here during war operations.

Beneath the flight deck is the gallery deck, housing the pilot's ready rooms and the air intelligence offices.

Also on the gallery deck is the Combat Information Center, the heart of the carrier during combat, which is jammed with electronics equipment and illuminated plotting boards. Various other air department spaces are here.

The hangar deck, the main deck of the ship, is where the aircraft are stored, repaired and maintained. Swift elevators raise the aircraft to the flight deck, lowering them again for maintenance and storage.

But the main stage of carrier air operations is the flight deck, which is divided into three sections:

Fly I—*launching area* under the direction of the Flight Deck Officer,

Fly II—*area amidships* under direction of the Flight Taxi Officer, and

Fly III—*landing area aft* under the direction of the Landing Signal Officer.

Flight operations on a carrier is a noisy, colorful ballet requiring the coordination of hundreds of men. The danger of handling rolling machinery, fueled with high-octane gas and usually loaded with explosives, requires speed, skill and great teamwork.

The whole deck becomes a panorama of color during takeoffs and landings. *Plane-handling crews,* which *spot* the planes, position them on the flight deck, and perform general duties, wear plain blue shirts. *Chockmen,* who handle the wooden chocks shoved under plane wheels to keep them from rolling, wear purple jerseys. *Taximen,* who direct and assist in taxiing the planes, wear yellow. *Hookmen,* whose job it is to dash out and disengage the plane's arrester hooks after it has landed, wear green. The plane engages the arresting cable in order to stop. *Fueling crews* wear red. Firefighters also wear red jerseys and red helmets. *Hot Poppas* are clad in asbestos suits in case they have to pull a pilot or crewman out of a burning aircraft.

In the heat of battle, planes come and go to refuel and rearm. For the first strike of the day, the three-place torpedo planes, the heaviest aircraft on the carriers, will be *spotted* furtherest aft because they require the longest takeoff runs. Next will be the scout or dive bombers, which are two-man planes (pilot and gunner-radioman). Finally, there are single-seat fighter planes, which usually take off first.

Before dawn fighter planes will be launched to provide a Combat Air Patrol (CAP) over the task force. In combat zones, this air umbrella stays above the carriers from sunrise to sunset, planes being relieved as they run low on fuel and pilots become weary.

The ready rooms with their comfortable, reclining, leather chairs are always the pre-strike nerve center, although pilots may sit here for hours before an action. They face a three-foot by three-foot screen on which teletype messages from the Combat Information Center reports of the enemy or other information. In the forward part of the low-ceilinged room is a blackboard on which up-to-date information is chalked: wind, course, speed, nearest land, etc.

Prior to a strike, the pilots are thoroughly briefed by the Air Combat Information Officer on the nature of the mission, their target and the expectation of enemy defenses. Squadron commanders brief the pilots on tactics to be used. Aerology will have prepared weather maps and provided advance information on weather conditions en route to and around the target. Each pilot has a small portable flight chart on which he records vital information that he will need in the cockpit.

When the loudspeaker orders, "Pilots, man your planes," the ready rooms empty and the pilots scramble up steel ladders, then run to their aircraft.

The carrier is steaming into the wind, adding its speed in order to give more lift to the planes as they take off. The white flying-flag breaks out from *Flag*

Control, and the yellow-clad Taximen wave the first aircraft in line to the take off spot.

There is always a moment of drama as the pilot awaits take off, sitting in his vibrating machine. He and his aircraft are the center of attention. In times of combat, those on the deck know that they might never see that aircraft or pilot again.

The Flight Deck Officer (Fly I) with a black and white checkered flag in hand then signals the pilot to open his throttle, "two block it." When the engine is wide open and howling, the aircraft quivering with restrained power, the flag whips down. The first plane releases its brakes, then thunders off, dipping slightly as it leaves the flight deck, and gains altitude. An efficient ship like the *Yorktown* will launch its entire air group in less than a half-hour, more than three planes off every minute.

Though the men who fly the carrier aircraft in this early May of 1942 would disagree, aviation is still very primitive. No one had heard of jet engines yet. There are no computers to navigate the aircraft, fire the machine guns or drop the bombs. Space flight and rockets belong to Buck Rogers in the comic strips. Ejection seats may be on someone's drawing board somewhere, but these pilots have to leave flaming aircraft the best way they can.

However, these aircraft sitting on the decks of the *Yorktown* and *Lexington* are sophisticated compared to the open cockpit biplanes of only a few years ago. The instrument panels do look imposing, and are compared to those of ten years ago. But in fact, the navigation instruments and engine performance gauges are still crude. Colonel Lindbergh's solo flight across the Atlantic Ocean was accomplished only fifteen years ago; the first aerial bombing only twenty-six years ago in London. The early pilots of World War I shot at each other with pistols in 1916; bombs were tossed out of cockpits by hand.

The pilots who will fly into the Coral Sea, most of them under twenty-four years of age, may have to "fly by the seat of their pants" to make it back to their carriers. Much has changed since Colonel Lindbergh's flight, but not enough.

6. The Preliminary

Of all the seas on earth, the warm blue Coral between the Solomon Islands and Australia's Great Barrier Reef may well be the most beautiful. Trade breezes caress the usually serene waters, and the winds of typhoons and hurricanes never lash it. Among its many islands are some true gems with dazzling white sand beaches, coconut palms and gentle brown inhabitants. Bombs had never exploded over the Coral Sea until yesterday—May 7, 1942.

The Japanese carriers *Zuikaku* and *Shokaku* sent air strikes against the American oiler *Neosho* and the destroyer *Sims*. Both were sunk with heavy loss of life. In turn, aircraft from the *Yorktown* and *Lexington* hit the Japanese light carrier *Shoho,* which was guarding the Port Moresby invasion transports. Exploding and burning furiously, the *Shoho* went under at full speed without launching any offensive strikes. The invasion transports turned back. Both actions, however, were only preliminary.

Today, May 8, marks the first time in history that heavy carrier forces have fought it out, waging a long-distance battle. The ships are never in sight of each other. There are no rules for this contest with the exception of "hit first," generally a sound practise in any battle. The odds, however, tend to favor the Japanese because of their pilots' experience, aircraft capability

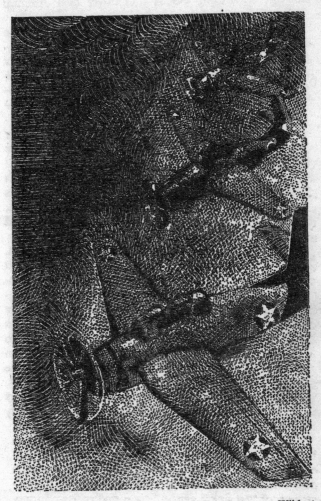

The U.S. Navy's Best Fighter Plane, The Grumman Wildcat

and the comforting clouds that hover over Admiral Takeo Takagi's ships.

The Japanese seem to have a definite edge on the Americans. The U.S. Navy's best fighter, the Grumman Wildcat, is somewhat outclassed by the enemy's Zero, a plane capable of 320 mph with a climb rate of 3,000 feet per minute, an important factor in protecting carriers. The Wildcat is slower in both categories.

Japan's best naval dive bomber, named "Val" by the U.S. forces, can carry twice the bomb load of the American SBD Dauntless and is faster.

Takagi's best torpedo plane, the Kate, can reach speeds up to 259 mph, and the Japanese torpedo is considered the world's best. The U.S. torpedo plane, the Douglas Devastator, is considerably slower and carries the world's most troublesome torpedo.

However, there are flaws in the Japanese aircraft, too. They lack sufficient armor to protect the pilots and fuel tanks. When the bullets begin to fly, the odds begin to even.

The Japanese pilots, at this point, are supposedly superior to the Americans. Having battled in China in the mid-1930s, they've had more experience. Both are certainly courageous, yet there is a difference in their air conduct as well as their tactics. The Japanese pilots often stunt or "make muscle" during dogfights, eager to show their flying ability. The American pilots are usually more interested in aiming guns properly than doing slow rolls.

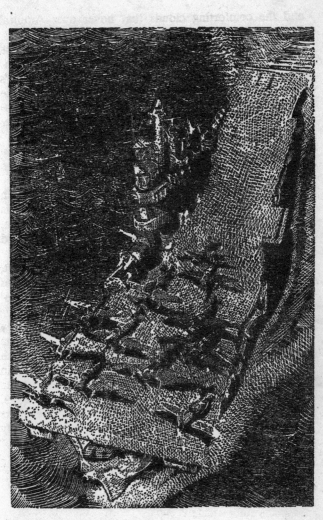

An Aircraft Carrier or Flattop

7. The Carriers Clash

Aerology on the *Lexington* has done its work well this early morning, and the pilots have complete up-to-date weather information, including direction and wind velocity at 1,000-foot levels specified for the maximum capacity of each aircraft. Weather to, from and over the target has been outlined. Every measure possible has been taken to get the pilots to target and then safely back to the home ship. They know the winds they'll have to buck and the clouds they'll drive through. Their fuel and distance are also calculated.

At about 6:30 A.M., "Lady Lex" launches Dauntless scout planes: Speed, 230 mph; range, about 1,000 miles. The scout bombers are manned by a pilot and a radioman-gunner.

Two hours later, a *Lexington* pilot finds the *Shokaku* and *Zuikaku,* partially hidden by clouds, 175 miles to the northeast, steaming along at twenty knots.

Almost simultaneously, a Japanese seaplane circles Task Force 17, and the American radio rooms intercept his priority message to Admiral Takagi. He is accurate in reporting the position, course and speed of the *Yorktown* and *Lexington.*

Admiral Fletcher now knows that he'll be attacked in less than two hours. Admiral Takagi faces the same prospects and begins to prepare for it.

The aircraft have been spotted for takeoff since dawn. Pilots of all four carriers are in their ready rooms, awaiting final information and word to "man your planes." Flight deck personnel are standing by as the carriers turn into the wind.

Admiral Takagi begins launching at 9 A.M. Soon sixty-nine Zero fighters, Val dive bombers and Kate torpedo planes are heading for the American ships, flying in *V* formations in stair-step divisions.

The *Yorktown* starts to launch a few minutes later, then the *Lexington*'s strike group is unchocked and rolling down the flight deck. Seventy-three Wildcat fighters, Dauntless dive bombers and Devastator torpedo planes are soaring toward the Japanese pilots.

These pilots know that in less than an hour they may spot enemy planes in the air, but no fighting will take place out here, midway between the two task forces. The dogfights will occur much closer to the carriers when the defensive CAPS dart in. Even if they pass each other close by, these opposing strike groups will not attack each other. Their mission is to destroy each others' ships.

There is a certain strangeness about this air battle. The admirals are no longer in control of events. At this point, they can only listen and wait, hope and pray. They know that in the few seconds that it takes for a bomb to tumble out of the sky, the tide of a battle can turn. The gun crews of both forces are standing by on their ships along with the damage-repair crews and the medical staffs.

The ships steam on in battle condition with all watertight doors and hatches "dogged"—closed and latched tight. There are five or six hundred separate compartments in a big carrier, and each one is an independent unit in case the next one is torn open by a bomb or torpedo.

Shortly before 11 A.M., emerging between holes in the clouds, the first of the *Yorktown*'s Dauntless dive bombers find the *Shokaku* and *Zuikaku,* each maneuvering to launch additional fighter planes. Their flight decks are painted bright yellow with the Japanese symbol of the "Rising Sun" a big red ball up forward.

The *Yorktown*'s slower Devastator torpedo planes arrive just as the *Zuikaku* slides into a rain squall to hide.

The dive bomber pilots and gunners make a last check, tighten their seat harnessing, then over they go at roughly seventy-degree angles, their dive flaps open at the trailing edges of the wings, their engines thundering. The rear-facing gunners scan around for Zeros as pilots stare intently at the "red ball" targets that grow larger and larger.

Zeros soar up to protect the sprinting flattops as torpedo planes from the *Yorktown* begin their low level runs on the *Shokaku*. The dive bombers get there first, scoring two hits. *Lexington* bombers score another hit, but the torpedo planes from both carriers fail miserably. Between the flashing Zeros and antiaircraft fire from the *Shokaku* and her escorts, American planes now begin to fall.

The dive bomber pilots are reaching down and forward with their left hands to release their explosives, and then pull up. But some don't. His plane on fire, Ensign "Jo-Jo" Powers drops his bomb at an altitude of 200 feet, then plunges straight into the ocean.

The wild and swift action is broken off in less than twenty minutes with pilots from the "Lady Lex" and *Yorktown* optimistically reporting back to Task Force 17 that they have left "one big carrier settling fast," sinking rapidly.

However, the *Shokaku* isn't settling fast *or* slow. She has shaken off the attacks, put her fires out, transfered many aircraft to the *Zuikaku,* and limps away. She is, nonetheless, severely damaged. The *Zuikaku,* still hiding in the heavy rain, comes through without a scratch.

Neither the *Yorktown* nor the *Lexington* have much to rejoice about despite the report of a big enemy carrier "settling fast." Out in the strong sunlight, the American flattops are taking their own licks. At

11:10, Japanese pilots make a brilliant run on the Lex, coming at her from both sides in a scissors tactic, releasing torpedoes about a half mile out. Two hit her squarely. She takes two more flight deck hits from the dive bomber attack.

Avoiding torpedoes, combing their wakes, guiding between the spearing trails of bubbles, the Yorktown takes a bomb hit on the flight deck near the carrier's island. The armor-piercing bomb drives a neat hole through the steel all the way down to the fourth deck, then explodes. The Yorktown survives it, although sixty-three men are lost.

The attack on both American ships is over within thirty minutes, a brief time considering that naval history is being made here. Aircraft have now taken the place of long-range guns.

The Japanese pilots head back for the crippled Shokaku and the Zuikaku; the American pilots return to Task Force 17. They will pass each other about midway between the two forces, but have no further taste for battle now, much less ammunition.

In Pearl Harbor Admiral Nimitz has followed all the action as best he can. Hypo's intercept stations have picked up messages from both sides—the reports from Japanese aircraft or ships, messages from Admiral Fletcher or between his ships. Operations Plot, in Nimitz's headquarters follows it on a big plotting board. The American forces are marked in blue, the Japanese in orange. Nimitz occasionally visits "Plot" to view the positions. Commander Rochefort's Black Chamber information is sent to Edwin Layton and then turned over to Operations Plot. Layton is continually informed of anything and everything that is pertinent to his command.

The Lexington, trailing smoke, steams on and begins to recover her aircraft though she is burning. Three boiler rooms are partially flooded. It appears that "Lady Lex" will survive, but at 12:47 P.M. gasoline vapors detonate, starting a series of fatal explosions.

Three hours later, her hull red-hot in places, she stops and Captain Ted Sherman passes orders for all hands to abandon ship. There is no panic. Ice cream from the ship's canteen is passed around. Ropes are lowered over the side. Some men decide to dive into the water, fitfy feet down. Others carefully line up shoes on the edge of the shattered flight deck, in an odd display of neatness, then jump.

Just before dark, the destroyer *U.S.S. Phelps* torpedoes the huge ship to render it completely useless. After a massive explosion, she convulses and slides under. Men weep openly.

As quiet returns to the Coral Sea, the *Yorktown* and her escorts, now laden with the survivors of the *Lexington,* depart the area, heading south. The Japanese steam away, too.

The final score of this first battle in naval history between aircraft carriers is difficult to assess. The Americans have downed the small *Shoho* and a destroyer, damaged the *Shokaku* enough to put her out of action for a while, destroyed seventy-seven Japanese aircraft and killed a number of experienced pilots. The Japanese forces have sunk the *Neosho,* the *Sims* and the *Lexington* and damaged the *Yorktown.* Thirty-eight planes from the *Yorktown* and *Lexington* are lost.

In terms of the overall war strategy, the Japanese invasion of Port Moresby has been turned back and will never be renewed. Australia is safe for the moment. In this respect, the Americans have won a clear victory.

But the Battle of Coral Sea is only a prelude, a warm-up and a testing for the larger, decisive battle to come.

8. Target Confirmed

As Hypo eavesdrops this first week of May, Admiral Nagumo sends a message to his carriers *Kaga* and *Hiryu,* and three escorting battleships. The admiral orders them to anchorages at Truk, a major naval base in the Caroline Islands. One of the battleships promptly replies to Nagumo, ". . . will be unable to accompany you on the campaign."

"What campaign? Where?" Joe Rochefort asks.

Rochefort and Layton begin to have second thoughts about Yamamoto's intentions. Up to this point they've been concentrating on the enemy's plans for the Port Moresby-Solomon Islands area. Now it appears that plans for an entirely different Japanese offensive are underway.

On May 6, another intriguing message is transmitted by the Japanese First Air Fleet to two carriers and three battleships. In the decoded message there is a reference to *AF,* and Black Chamber workers believe that it might refer to a Central Pacific destination. The Japanese have frequently used two initials to identify a place or operation. *MO* meant Moresby, for example. The single letter "A" seemed to indicate mid-Pacific. *AH* was the Pearl Harbor code designation for Nagumo's Hawaii attack.

Several of the Hypo staff recall seeing a designation similar to *AF* recently. A check of the piles of past decoded intercepts finally produces one with *AG* in the text. Those initials were first used in March in refer-

ence to the French Frigate Shoals, not far from
Midway. Submarines rendezvoused with long-range reconnaisance flying boats at the Shoals to refuel them
(planes refueled, not subs).

If *AH* meant Pearl Harbor, and *AG* meant the
French Frigate Shoals, then *AF* was quite possibly
Midway. It probably is Midway, Rochefort and
Layton finally decide. Layton informs Admiral Nimitz,
and while CINCPAC is inclined to agree, he points
out that both Washington experts and Army commanders in Hawaii have other ideas about Japan's
next offensive.

Washington intelligence officers maintain that the
South Pacific will remain the area of action. They
downgrade Midway. The Army command in Hawaii
steadfastly clings to a Japanese attack on Oahu. The
Army Air Force selects San Francisco as Yamamoto's
next destination with a stopover in Hawaii.

Proof that *AF* is Yamamoto's actual target is des-
perately needed, and deception is the only way to at-
tain that proof. Rochefort and Layton arrange for
Midway to send a "plain language" routine message to
Pearl Harbor, saying that the base is low on fresh water. They know the uncoded message will be monitored
in Tokyo.

The Japanese bite. A few days later, Hypo decodes
a routine Japanese transmission passing on information
to interested commands that *"AF* has fresh water
problems."

There is a moment of triumph in Rochefort's office
and in CINCPAC intelligence. Rochefort and Layton
now have absolute proof that *AF* refers to Sand and
Eastern atolls. Nimitz now fully accepts their estimation, and alerts all commands—*Midway is the next
target*. He guesses as to the time of attack, late May
or early June.

Until the Coral Sea battle, Nimitz and his staff had
been rather confident of winning any carrier fight
against the Japanese despite the enemy's superior
numbers and advantage in pilot experience. Nimitz

fully believed in the determination of the American pilots, and thought his task force commanders could outsmart the enemy. However, with the *Lexington* sunk and the *Yorktown* damaged from that single bomb hit, CINCPAC is not quite so optimistic now. He has the *Enterprise* and the *Hornet,* perhaps the *Yorktown,* to oppose as many as ten Japanese flattops.

Whatever the odds, Nimitz is counting heavily on a surprise attack on Nagumo's carriers before the enemy troop ships are within sight of the island. He also hopes that Yamamoto will believe that he intends to attack the enemy *after* Midway has been captured, not before.

In some ways, Nimitz himself is a captive of the intelligence reports. Everything is based on the Black Chamber's ability to read enemy intentions from the JN-25 messages. If they are misread, or worse, if they are part of a grand deception staged by Yamamoto, CINCPAC faces the possible loss of the Central Pacific—perhaps the loss of the war. With these fears in mind, Nimitz assigns a tough-minded, nagging officer, Captain J.M. Steele to question Rochefort and Layton at every turn and go over again and again each estimation.

Finally, Rochefort and Layton tell CINCPAC that the Japanese Combined Fleet will be divided into a Northern Force to invade the Aleutian Islands as a diversion, a Midway Invasion Force and the First Carrier Strike Force. They even predict the exact islands for the Aleutian diversionary landings—Kiska, Adak and Attu. They then provide a numerical estimate of the forces they think Admiral Yamamoto will send into the Central Pacific—four carriers, two to four battleships, eight or nine heavy cruisers, fifteen to twenty destroyers, two submarine squadrons and an estimated 15,000 troops aboard the transports.

No other military campaign in any war has ever been foretold in such detail, and many of the officers on Nimitz's staff, who are unaware that JN-25 has been broken, believe that the Japanese are playing games with naval intelligence, and that Rochefort and Layton are out of their minds. Only a few high-ranking officers in Pearl Harbor and Washington know JN-25 has been compromised.

Nimitz is still worried. On May 24, he summons Joe Rochefort to his office. Perhaps CINCPAC and his suspicious staff officers can shake the Black Chamber man. They have many questions to ask, but Commander Rochefort does not arrive at the appointed hour. The clock ticks on. Few naval officers would dare be late for an appointment with CINCPAC, but Rochefort shows up thirty minutes past the hour, looking worn-out, disheveled and displaying a growth of whiskers. He explains to his commander in chief that he's been up all night working with his code people.

"We can say when the enemy will strike," says Rochefort. *"Aleutians, June 3. Midway, June 4."*

The anger of Admiral Chester Nimitz ebbs quickly. He summons Commander Layton next.

For some time, Nimitz has told Layton to put himself in the shoes of Admiral Yamamoto, to think as Yamamoto thinks, to plan as Yamamoto plans, to act as Yamamoto acts. Now Nimitz orders Layton to use this background, gather all his data, think it over, and make one final estimate of the coming attack. No estimate ever made by naval intelligence is as crucial as this one. Layton begins to review everything that he and Rochefort have discovered since early May. He examines all the pertinent intercepts again, especially those having to do with *AF*. He checks navigational charts, discusses possibilities with Operations, confers almost hourly with Joe Rochefort. Neither man gets more than three or four hours sleep a night.

Finally, Nimitz becomes impatient and demands an answer. Time is crucial. The most critical day of the entire war may be June 4, just two weeks away. Layton, claiming he doesn't want to be specific, is very specific. *The Japanese will come in from the north-*

*west on bearing 325 degrees. They'll be sighted about
175 miles from Midway on June 4 at about 6* A.M.

Nimitz thanks his weary and worried intelligence
officer and promptly puts the new information to work.
Ed Layton is guardedly confident. There is always the
possibility that the Japanese are sending out false messages simply to trick the Pearl Harbor command.

9. The Carriers Sail

Aboard the *Yamato,* still at fleet anchorage, on this twenty-fifth day of May (the 24th in Honolulu), the Midway and Aleutian operations are being rehearsed on table-top charts, with models of the ships being positioned with long sticks. As in their prior games, the Japanese always seem to win. Today, the referee, who is a commander, rules that two of the Imperial Navy carriers have been sunk in action. Yamamoto's chief of staff promptly overrules the commander and "refloats" one of the flattops. A little later, Rear Admiral Matome Ugaki "refloats" the other one. This action by Ugaki is indicative of the military ailment that Yamamoto most fears—"victory fever," also called arrogant overconfidence.

This same day, Yamamoto's intelligence officers brief him on American capabilities at Midway. They predict that there are about 750 well-trained Marines for ground defense, about twenty-four Catalina-type seaplanes for reconnaisance, twelve Army bombers and twenty Navy or Marine Corps fighter aircraft. Their estimate is fairly accurate for this day.

As for the U.S. carriers, Japanese intelligence experts tell Yamamoto that the *Enterprise* and the *Hornet* have returned to Pearl Harbor after the Tokyo raid and that one of the two carriers (*Yorktown* and *Lexington*) believed to have been sunk in the Coral Sea may only have been badly damaged. The *Enterprise* and the *Hornet* haven't returned yet. Otherwise, the report is quite accurate.

Early that evening, some two hundred officers from the ships at anchor at Hashirajima, including force commanders and staff officers, resplendent in their white dress uniforms with their war medals flashing on their chests, gather aboard the *Yamato* to join their commander in chief in toasting to the success of the Midway invasion. Yamamoto sips tea while his officers drink the traditional rice wine called *sake*. Tonight's wine is very special, a gift from the Emperor. The festivities are appropriate for the *Yamato*. The steel monster will be making her maiden voyage into action, and her men take it for granted that she'll easily defeat any American ship that happens to come her way.

Two days later, the dawn at Hashirajima anchorage is clear and warm. The sun shines off the small yellow tugboats that dart around the great roadstead, winding between the larger gray ships that lie low in the water, heavy with fuel and explosives.

It is Japanese Navy Day, anniversary of Admiral Togo's momentous victory over the Russian fleet thirty-seven years earlier—an appropriate day for Admiral Nagumo's heavy carriers to sail for Midway. Precisely at 8 A.M., a flag breaks out from the *Akagi*'s signal mast—*Sortie as scheduled.*

The twenty-one ships of Nagumo's First Carrier Force have been prepared for hours. The only tasks left are to heave in their anchors or slip their mooring lines from the buoys. Within a few minutes, the sleek warriors of Destroyer Division 10 are underway. They'll pace ahead and around the carriers. Next are the cruisers, then the battleships *Haruna* and *Kirishima,* finally the heavy carriers *Akagi, Kaga, Hiryu,* and *Soryu.* Sailors line their decks and respond to the cheers from the ships temporarily left behind.

Admiral Yamamoto watches the spectacle from his flagship. He'll be following soon.

Also watching the outbound parade from the *Akagi*'s bridge are Lieutenant Commander Mitsuo

Fuchida and his friend, Commander Minoru Genda. Fuchida had led the Pearl Harbor attack which was planned by the foxy strategist, Genda. For the Midway attack Fuchida again will fly the lead aircraft and Genda will stay by the side of Nagumo on the flag bridge to offer advice.

The stocky, balding Nagumo is not an aviator, and his naval commands had stepped up the usual route —destroyers to cruisers to battleships. He'd taken command of the heavy carriers in 1941. When he was a younger officer with the rank of captain, he'd impressed both Genda and Fuchida as being a good leader and an aggressive fighter. However, they've noticed a change in the admiral lately. He seems cautious and indecisive, hardly ever questioning Genda's plans. Perhaps age is catching up with Chuichi Nagumo. The admiral's performance at Pearl Harbor is very fresh in Genda's memory. The admiral had refused to allow a second strike to be launched against the American naval base to destroy fuel supplies and submarine facilities. Nagumo was playing it safe. Too safe in Genda's opinion.

The carriers are all underway within twenty minutes, forming a column for departure. Remaining in the anchorage are the vessels of Battleship Division 1 and 2, which will be personally commanded by Admiral Yamamoto. The seven dreadnoughts are clustered south of the departing carriers. They'll sail in forty-eight hours.

Soon the First Carrier Force, veteran of air strikes from Oahu to the Indian Ocean, files proudly down the Bungo Channel, then passes out of the Inland Sea into the rolling blue Pacific at about noon, quickly maneuvering into steaming formation—the *Akagi* and the *Kaga* in one column, the *Hiryu* and the *Soryu* in another, their escorts spread around them guarding against submarine attack. Their speed is twenty knots; course is set to the east.

10. Operation Plan 29–42

Nagumo's ships are almost a day out of Japan when Vice Admiral William Halsey, ailing from a painful skin disease, brings Task Force 16, *Enterprise* and *Hornet,* up the Pearl Harbor channel for two days of round-the-clock provisioning and refueling. The aircraft that could be flown off the two flattops are already ashore. Those that cannot fly will be lifted off by crane for hurried maintenance or replacement. "Bull" Halsey is in a foul, despairing mood, suspecting that he might be sent ashore to miss what will surely be a crucial battle. He's a fighter, but he hasn't done very well against acute dermatitis. Itching and scratching, he hasn't been able to sleep very much for more than a week and has lost weight. Nerves frayed, the admiral who has led the Pacific offensive thus far reports to Nimitz and is promptly ordered into the hospital. He complains, but CINCPAC won't listen. Halsey then nominates Rear Admiral Raymond Spruance, commander of Task Force No. 16's cruiser screen, to be his temporary replacement.

This is a rather surprising choice by Halsey. Spruance is a "black shoe," gunnery man, not an aviator, and not at all like the bold, vocal Halsey. Short and lean with a crew cut, the quiet and unassuming Spruance completely lacks Halsey's flair for drama. He does not create headlines. However, Raymond Spruance is a top officer, and will likely make few mistakes. He's a safe commander for the job ahead. Nimitz quickly approves of Halsey's selection.

The admirals discuss what lies ahead and agree that the best strategy is to take the U.S. carriers northeast of Midway and wait, letting the long-range search planes from Midway, the Catalinas, seek out the enemy approach. They agree that the best possible tactic is to form a flanking position off to the side of the Nagumo carriers, then take the Japanese by surprise. In the words of Nimitz, ". . . blow them to hell."

CINCPAC is wagering that the Japanese have no idea that he knows almost as much about MI Operation as they do, thanks to the decoded JN-25, Rochefort and Layton. To secure his bet, Nimitz has ordered another deceptive measure in the South Pacific. When the *Hornet* and *Enterprise* raced for home in response to Nimitz's orders, after having been purposely sighted around the Solomon Islands, the seaplane tender *Tangier*, her patrol bombers and the cruiser *Salt Lake City* began faking messages for the two carriers, making it appear that they were still operating in the area.

This type of ruse is not new. The Japanese, in fact, used it just before Pearl Harbor, fooling Ed Layton. Genda had ships in the Inalnd Sea sending messages as if they came from the heavy carriers, which were actually already nearing Pearl Harbor. But the tables are turned now, and the Naval General Staff in Tokyo are convinced that Halsey's carriers are still in the South Pacific.

One admiral, however, is not so sure—Yamamoto. His own intelligence officers at the fleet anchorage note the extremely heavy communications traffic that is being intercepted from Pearl Harbor.

"Why is this happening?" he asks. No one can tell him.

The day after Halsey comes into port feeling miserable, the only other operable U.S. carrier in the Pacific is the *Yorktown*, which is trailing oil from her bomb rupture received in the Coral Sea battle. She takes tugs off Oahu, and soon steams slowly up the channel to the whistle blasts of the ships in port. There are cheers from those standing on shore. She's a wounded war veteran and noses into the "hospital," Dry Dock 1 at the Navy Yard.

The *Yorktown* has been at sea 102 days. Under normal circumstances she is due for some overhaul time; some rest and recreation for her crew. Repair of the bomb damage would usually take at least ninety days. However, Nimitz, in rubber boots, wading at the bottom of Dry Dock I to inspect the hull personally, lets it be known that he wants the *Yorktown* back in the water in less than *ninety hours*. She is allotted exactly three days for temporary repairs, and the loading of stores, ammunition and fuel.

Within an hour, navy yard workmen are lighting up cutting and welding torches to begin temporary repair of the *Yorktown*'s bomb damage. The hull will be patched, but there isn't time for needed engine work. More than a thousand workmen are aboard the *Yorktown.*

In the afternoon, the quaint railroad cars of the Oahu Railway Company are lifted onto the flight deck to begin unloading supplies. There is little shore leave for officers and crew, and work details go on through the night.

In the evening, armed couriers move around the Naval Base, the yard and fleet anchorage by jeep and by boat, distributing the Top Secret CINCPAC Operation Plan 29-42, the detailed instructions for fighting the Japanese at Midway. Eighty-six copies of the document are delivered to various ships and commands. Tasks are assigned to each vessel, dovetailing the ground and air defenses of Midway to the sea forces that will operate to the northeast.

At this point, only the very senior commanders know what is about to happen. Due to the frantic preparations, most officers and crews of the ships and commands involved have already guessed that "something big" is about to occur. They still have no idea what, when or where. Secrecy, that ultimate weapon of war, has been maintained.

On this night of May 28, Rear Admiral Frank Jack Fletcher, who had hoped for a rest for his ships, crews, perhaps even himself, prepares to take over command off Midway. He is senior to Spruance, who will fly his flag from the *Enterprise*.

But the "Big E" and the *Hornet* do not wait for Fletcher and the *Yorktown*. They'll meet the dry-docked carrier later on at sea. On May 29, they slip lines and move out down Pearl Channel, joining their escort of six cruisers and nine destroyers off Oahu. The screen of ships form a circle as the flattops begin to receive their air groups. When the *Hornet*'s planes are all snugged down, wings folded, Captain Marc "Pete" Mitscher's voice blares from the speaker system, "This is the captain. We are going to intercept a Jap attack on Midway." He has always been a man of few words.

At last, the remaining Japanese ships at Hashirajima are underway. The Midway invasion force, a support group of cruisers, two battleships, eight destroyers and the light carrier *Zuiho* are passing through Bungo Strait and will head east. Immediately following these ships are Yamamoto's Main Body of thirty-two units, including seven battleships, the light carrier *Hosho*, two cruisers and twenty-one destroyers. They swing southeast at a brisk eighteen knots.

As of noon May 29, the largest naval force in history is spread over hundreds of miles at sea, heading for the North and Central Pacific Ocean. With the Aleutian invasion forces and the submarines heading toward Pearl Harbor hoping to torpedo departing U.S. ships, more than 150 Japanese naval units are on the prowl.

Although Yamamoto has a siege of stomach cramps,

the spirits of most of the men in the armada are high. They are singing battle songs, certain that they are about to be involved in a great victory. However, the Japanese will lose the first silent encounter of the battle off Midway Island this day.

Japanese submarines I-121 and I-123 are safely in position off the French Frigate Shoals near Midway, waiting to refuel the long-range seaplanes that will make a reconnaisance of Pearl Harbor and report back to Admiral Yamamoto the crucial absence or presence of American aircraft carriers. This mission has been designated Operation K by Yamamoto's planners—"K" standing for the Kawanishi flying boats that are being used.

But much to the dismay of the sub commanders, frustrating changes have taken place at the once-deserted French Frigate Shoals. Nimitz had it occupied simply to thwart Operation K, whatever its purpose. Once again, JN-25 has provided the important information that allows Nimitz to stall the enemy. Two U.S. Navy seaplane tenders now ride at anchor less than a quarter-mile from the subs. In March, when the Japanese operation was first tried, only sea birds were seen around the reef. The sub skippers scan the ships constantly through their periscopes, hoping they'll leave by the next day when the Kawanishi flying boats are scheduled to arrive and refuel en route to Pearl Harbor.

The *Ballard* and *Thornton* remain, however. They're just sitting. The crews are puzzled as to why they are at these godforsaken shoals, doing absolutely nothing. And they have no idea that they're being watched by enemy subs.

The last major contestant from the American side, the hastily and temporarily repaired *Yorktown,* floats free of Dry Dock 1 at the Navy Yard at 9 A.M., May 30. Swinging around, she heads down the channel with a brace of tugs keeping her steady. The cruiser and destroyer escorts are already at sea.

Seventy-six aircraft soon line the *Yorktown*'s flight deck. By nightfall the big carrier is headed for Point Luck, the rendezvous spot. She'll meet up with the *Hornet* and the *Enterprise* at 32° north latitude, 173° west longitude—325 miles northeast of Midway.

11. Work and Wait

Much of Midway is now underground. Dugouts and slit trenches are everywhere. The hospital is underground. There are underground bunkers to store supplies, ammunition, and even aircraft. Near the center of Sand Island is the new command post, also beneath the earth's surface.

Although much has already been done, Midway is still in the heat of preparing for the enemy. Barbed wire is coiled and wound over the white sand beaches. Out in the water beyond the surf are electronically controlled mines that will explode at the touch of a button. There also are hastily placed underwater obstacles—steel and concrete barriers to stop the progress of enemy landing craft. Gunnery positions now ring the atoll, and one has to be careful where one steps or swims. Instant death can be the result of carelessness.

On May 18, 1942, Nimitz had written a letter to the Midway commanders, Navy Captain Cyril Simard and Marine Colonel Harold Shannon, informing them of Yamamoto's immediate plans against their island base. Nimitz went into considerable detail for the joint commanders, both tough and tenacious veterans of World War I.

On May 23, the cruiser *U.S.S. St. Louis* dropped by to disembark two rifle companies of Major Evan Carlson's newly formed Second Raider Battalion. These are "different" Marines, patterned after the British commando units, trained in hand-to-hand combat, and equipped with belts of grenades and razor-sharp Bowie knives. They looked as ferocious as Major Carlson had intended. They were most welcome on Sand Island.

Next day, the *U.S.S. Kittyhawk,* a converted railway ferry, stood into the small harbor to off-load defense batteries, light tanks, eighteen dive bombers and seven fighter aircraft. Also coming ashore from the *Kitty Hawk* were twenty-one bewildered pilots, most of them fresh out of flight school. They didn't understand why they'd been shipped to Midway. But Captain Simard quickly informs them, "The Japs are coming!" Ten torpedo boats then arrive from the Hawaiian sea frontier, fine craft for night attacks on enemy troop transports.

Nimitz's promise for more air support is fulfilled with twelve additional PBY Catalinas, four Army B-26 bombers and seventeen B-17s, which are the Army's long-range bombers. And arriving on this first day of June to complete the air arm are six new TBF Avengers, Grumman torpedo planes now being introduced to the fleet. These belong to the *Hornet*'s Torpedo Squadron 8, but having been in training, they missed the carrier's departure from Pearl Harbor. These new torpedo planes are larger and have more power than the Devastators.

As the Avengers land on Eastern this afternoon, they bring Midway's air strength to 121 combat planes. Tents are set up around many of the parked aircraft. There aren't enough accommodations for all the visitors from Hawaii. Midway's population is now almost 3,000 officers and enlisted men. The island has shifted from a completely defensive stance to one of offense as well.

But both Simard and Shannon are realistic and acknowledge that it is possible the Japanese will capture Sand and Eastern. Therefore, they lay careful plans to destroy everything the Japanese can use. The secret communication codes have already been shipped back to Pearl Harbor. Demolition charges have been placed throughout both islands. In fact, during an unscheduled demolition rehearsal the past week, a sailor crossed the wrong wires and blew up 400,000 gallons of aviation gas. Aircraft fueling will now have to be done by hand pump, the long hard way. A freighter, the *Nira Luckenback,* is visiting this balmy Sunday, off-loading drums of fuel to replace the exploded high test.

Enemy eyes are watching all this activity from the sea. Submarine *I-168* is at periscope depth off Midway and reports to the Combined Fleet headquarters in the *Yamato* that the Americans seem to be flying patrols to the southwest, probably to a distance of some 600 miles away, judging from the length of time that the planes are gone each day. Lieutenant Commander Yahachi Tanabe, skipper of the *I-168,* estimates that more than twenty of the Catalinas are flying in the daily searches.

Tanabe also informs Yamamoto's staff that he believes an alert is in effect on the island. His reports are decoded in the *Yamato* and shown to the commander in chief, but the information, which might indicate that the Americans are aware of advancing ships and that surprise has been lost, is not transmitted on to Admiral Nagumo. Nor does Yamamoto tell Nagumo that Japanese intercept stations have noticed a huge increase in "urgent" messages sent out from CINCPAC, another telltale sign that the element of surprise may have been lost and that Nimitz is preparing for some kind of large scale action. Moreover, information that American submarines have been spotted in several areas about 500 miles from Wake Island is withheld from Nagumo. The sightings could indicate that a submarine patrol line, intended to sight and attack the Japanese fleet, has been set up by Nimitz.

Despite all this evidence, Yamamoto and his staff —especially the meditating, chain-smoking planner,

Captain Kurashima—cling stubbornly to the belief that they will catch the Americans off guard once again as they did December 7. To inform Nagumo of the Midway air patrols and the sub sightings, Yamamoto would be forced to break radio silence. American intercept operators could monitor the Japanese transmissions and pinpoint Yamamoto's position at sea as he advanced toward Midway. Kurashima insists that breaking radio silence would alert the Americans to the entire operation, giving them several days to prepare defenses. The mystic with the shaven head also assumes that Admiral Nagumo has heard Tanabe's transmissions on his own radios. Kurashima does not know that the radio receivers in the *Akagi* are inferior and that Nagumo's operators haven't received a single dot or dash from the *I-168*.

Yamamoto, taking Kurashima's advice, remains silent as his Main Body, cruising 600 miles behind the carriers, slugs through heavy seas and driving rain.

Admiral Nagumo, enclosed in thick fog, with his ships in danger of collision, is not even aware that Operation K, the flying boat reconnaisance on Pearl Harbor, has been cancelled. The Kawanishi seaplanes can't land at the French Frigate Shoals to refuel because the *Thornton* and *Ballard* are still anchored there. Nor does Nagumo know that the Japanese submarines scheduled to keep watch on the seaplanes off Pearl Harbor and pass the word when the "American fleet sails to defend Midway" are not yet on station.

On this tense, foggy day, June 3, (Tokyo time,) an uneasy Nagumo turns to his staff in angry frustration, asking, "But where is the enemy fleet? Have they sailed or haven't they?"

The senior member, Captain Oishi replies, in part, ". . . if his [Nimitz] forces are now in Pearl Harbor, we shall have plenty of time to prepare for them should they sortie following our strike on Midway. They will have over 1,000 miles to cover."

Down below and out of the chill mist sweeping over the flight deck, the *Akagi*'s pilots laugh, joke and play cards to pass the time. The mood on all the ships remains supremely confident, though the crusty Nagumo continues to worry.

Compounding the many other mistakes of the day, the Naval General Staff in Tokyo sends a comforting message to Yamamoto during the afternoon, *"Enterprise* and *Hornet* remain in the Solomon Islands area."* The Tokyo operators keep intercepting the phony transmissions from the "carrier pilots to their ships." In the *Yamato* flag operations room, Kurashima says, "You see, there is nothing to worry about."

Midway's air patrols are indeed fanning out, not the 600 miles that Tanabe estimated, but 700 miles and more. They are taking off at dawn, searching for the Japanese ships, covering an area much larger than the mere reported "southwest." The PBY's are hunting in a westerly semicircle from south of the island to north of it. No enemy ships have been sighted as yet, but already two of the Catalinas have returned home peppered with bullets from Japanese Zeros stationed on Wake Island. There is air contact with the enemy at least once a day, including this day. June 2, Midway time.

Finally the *Hornet* and the *Enterprise,* believed by Tokyo to be in the Solomons, have met the *Yorktown* at "Point Luck," 325 miles northeast of Midway. The three carriers now steam back and forth, waiting patiently for Admiral Nagumo.

12. Do You See What I See?

Dawn light is expected to reach Midway about 4 A.M. on this warm morning of June 3, but the Pratt & Whitney engines of the PBYs are already roaring. Exhaust swirls in the light breeze, and the navigational lights blink from the row of planes. Pilots, crewman and mechanics have been up for almost two hours. The first Catalina is airborne at 4:15 A.M. Within twelve minutes, more than twenty of the amphibious aircraft have lifted and vanished to the west into the darkness.

Then louder roars from the four-engined Army B-17s are heard from the Eastern strip. The Army planes will take off and circle well away from the atoll until the PBYs, reaching a distance of 400 miles on the spokes of their search, radio that all is safe, no enemy carriers are in sight. The big bombers can return to Eastern without danger of being caught on the ground and destroyed in a surprise raid.

The twin-engined Catalinas are about as graceful as the gooney birds they have just disturbed, yet they are ideal aerial observation platforms. With their huge gas tanks they can stay aloft all day, having a range of 3000 miles. The Navy has no other long-range search planes better suited for sea hunts, and the molasses-slow PBYs are proving to be invaluable.

Unfortunately, they are also easy targets for enemy fighter planes. Aside from reconnaisance, the Catalinas have limited bomber ability, and can drop depth charges on submarines. Infrequently, they are out-

The Zero Taking Off From A Carrier Flight Deck

The Twin-Engined Catalina

fitted with torpedos. Their main job is to look down upon miles of mostly vacant ocean.

The area that Ensign Jack Reid has been assigned to search this morning is the probable path of the Japanese invasion force, according to Commander Layton's estimate. Reid won the right to search this particular choice sector by drawing the longest straw from his skipper's hand. His fellow pilots are off searching less likely expanses.

At 8:40 AM. Reid is at the very bottom of his search arc and hasn't seen anything other than birds, splashing fish and small whitecaps. But since he did have the luck of drawing the "long straw," he decides to drone on another ten or fifteen minutes just in case. A few minutes after nine, his decision pays off.

"Do you see what I see?" he asked his copilot, Ensign Hardeman. With his binoculars Reid has picked up specks on the horizon, and smoke seems to be coming from them.

"You're damn right, I do," answers Hardeman, staring ahead. The "specks" are about thirty miles away.

Reid radios back to Midway, *"Am investigating suspicious vessels."*

Hearts beat a little faster in the command post on Sand Island and on Eastern, where the B-17s are parked on the air strip ready for immediate takeoff and bombing runs. Colonel Shannon and Captain Simard wait it out as tension mounts on both islands. There is little doubt that Reid has sighted the enemy.

The slow, cumbersome Catalina takes twenty minutes to reach the vicinity of the convoy. Reid then makes his confirmation, "Main body"—a startling message.

Hearing the transmission in Pearl Harbor, Rochefort and Layton react negatively. It is very doubtful that Ensign Reid has sighted the "Main Body," Yamamoto's battleships and escorts. Perhaps Reid has made contact with the troop ships.

Reid and Hardeman begin to track the force, dodging in and out of the low clouds, attempting to keep away from the antiaircraft fire, which is often heavy but not accurate. The job now is to identify the ships by type, if possible; count them, then estimate their course and speed.

At about 11:00 A.M., Reid clarifies his second report, ". . . eleven ships, making nineteen knots eastward." Reid has discovered the transport group, but his count is wrong. There are, in fact, twelve transports, three destroyer transports, ten destroyers and the light cruiser *Jintsu*. It is difficult to make precise observations while dodging gunfire, dashing from cloud to cloud. Usually, the observer sees more ships, rather than less; reports more damage, rather than less. Nonetheless, Reid has located and successfully tracked the enemy convoy for an hour and thirty minutes. Preparing to order an attack on the ships, Captain Simard summons Reid home. A job well done!

Army Air Force Colonel Walter Sweeney has been anxious to take off ever since the ensign's first report. His B-17s are armed with four 600-pound bombs each and have extra gas tanks for the long flight. Sweeney would dearly love to have the U.S. Army, rather than the Navy, break up the Midway invasion. Service rivalry, of course, is always strong. Simard gives Sweeney the okay after Reid's last message and the AAF bombers begin to move down Eastern's air strip at 12:30 P.M., the colonel personally in command. Having been stationed at Hickam Field, Hawaii, the Army pilots have only dropped bombs in target practice. They are now spoiling for a real fight.

As the B-17s roll up and away, Admiral Yamamoto, still pitching and tossing in heavy seas with his battleships, is digesting a disturbing message from the cruiser *Jintsu*. "*Attack on troop transports is anticipated.*" No one expected that the transports would be discovered before Nagumo's carriers could strike Midway. The first hint of trouble for *Operation MI* comes from the *Jintsu's* startling message.

Almost five hours later, anticipation ends with the delivery of the 600-pound bombs from Colonel Sweeney's B-17s. They represent the first blows of the battle off Midway Island. Led by the *Jintsu,* the two columns of enemy ships twist and turn to avoid being hit deliberately, spouting heavy smoke to confuse the bombardiers. Their antiaircraft fire falls short of the highflying 17s.

The strike on the transports is over in a few minutes, and Sweeney, watching the explosions below, is certain that his squadron has made hits. He reports back to Midway, ". . . damage to two battleships or heavy cruisers, plus two transports." Sweeney is positive that he saw two of the ships "stopped dead and smoking heavily." It takes years to convince him otherwise. Not a single hit was made by his bombers. The 600-pounders had blown up on impact with the water. The Army Air Force soon learned the problems of hitting zigzagging ships from high altitudes.

At twilight four PBYs struggle into the air from the strip on Eastern, each carrying a single torpedo. These planes are manned by exhausted pilots and crew members, all volunteers. They've flown out from Oahu as a "special attack group" and have been in the air all day. Simard tells them that they don't have to go, but tomorrow might be too late. And after all, they've come all this way for just one reason, an attempt to torpedo enemy ships. The weary pilots vote unanimously to go.

Three of the four amphibians reach the transport group at about 1:30 A.M., first making radar contact, then spotting the two columns of blacked out ships in the moonlight. They are leaving long trails of silvery wakes, making them comparatively easy to see.

The lead Catalina begins its run, drops the torpedo,

then thunders over an enemy ship, barely clearing it. There is a flash. The oiler *Akebono Maru* is hit. The other PBYs unfortunately don't score. The exhausted PBY pilots head home to Midway, about 500 miles east.

Although the postmidnight attack is not successful, Yamamoto is now given notice that his ships can be under fire night or day. The *Jintsu* reports to him that the oiler is damaged, but will probably survive.

The day has been long and tense for everyone. There is a certainty that if the battle didn't begin today, it will tomorrow. At CINCPAC headquarters, Admiral Nimitz dozes on a cot after leaving orders to awaken him if anything important develops. Down in the Black Chamber, though it is 2 A.M., Joe Rochefort is at work, studying decoded intercepts. He's brought his battle helmet to work for the first time since the war began because of the remote possibility of an air raid.

Above ground a red alert is in effect. The Navy Yard is completely blacked out, as is the Naval Base and all other military installations on Oahu. A blackout is in effect in Honolulu. All antiaircraft guns are manned.

All service leaves have been cancelled on the West Coast of the United States from Seattle to San Diego. The Army has ordered an alert in the San Francisco area. They are still convinced that the city by the Golden Gate is the enemy's primary target.

Nerves are also on edge on the American task forces now closing on Midway. Admiral Fletcher plans to have the *Enterprise,* the *Hornet* and *Yorktown* in position about 200 miles off the island at dawn, on the Japanese flank and ready for aircraft launching. He and Admiral Spruance have waited for word of sightings all day, hoping that someone flying an aircraft or looking through a sub periscope would spot

Nagumo and his flattops. The hours have dragged maddeningly.

On the *Hornet* pilots and air crews were up at 1 A.M. for breakfast and briefings, then kept in a state of readiness until late afternoon. It has been a wearisome, frustrating day with a number of false alarms. Several times the Navy pilots manned their planes only to be returned to the ready rooms. There were more briefings. Communications procedures were rechecked. Planes were checked over again, mechanics fussing and fine-tuning them.

The *Hornet*'s Torpedo 8 boss is skinny, savage John C. Waldron, a lieutenant commander. He never calls a torpedo by its proper name. He prefers "wienie" or "pickle." Waldron, who wears a long hunting knife as well as a .45 calibre pistol on his web belt, gave out a mimeographed message to his pilots this day:

> Just a word to let you know I feel we are all ready. We have had a very short time to train, and we have worked under the most severe difficulties. But we have truly done the best humanly possible. I actually believe that under these conditions we are the best in the world. My greatest hope is that we encounter a favorable tactical situation, but if we don't and worst come to worst, I want each of us to do his utmost to destroy our enemies. If there is only one plane left to make a final run in, I want that man to go in and get a hit. May God be with us all. Good luck, happy landings and give 'em hell.

John Waldron's message and Torpedo 8 are destined to become famous.

Other messages are passed. Speeches are made by squadron commanders on the other carriers. But with all the fine speeches and brave words comes the hard knowledge that within twenty-four hours some of those bright young faces in the ready rooms and in the crew's mess will not be there. That is not discussed.

Meanwhile, the pilots and air crews of the *Hornet,* the *Enterprise* and the *Yorktown* are being awakened. It is 2 A.M. June 4, 1942.

13. Enemy Carriers

All the elements for a major battle, one that will perhaps change the whole course of the war, are moving relentlessly into place as darkness begins to flee the Central Pacific on this June 4. The gray shapes of Admiral Nagumo's carriers, *Akagi, Soryu, Hiryu* and *Kaga,* are steaming steadily toward his desired aircraft launch point, 230 miles northwest of Midway. He plans to begin launching about 4:30 A.M., thirty minutes from now. His planes, which will bomb and strafe Midway, are "running up," warming their engines. The noise is deafening. The flattops of Admirals Fletcher and Spruance are also gliding along in the thin, early light roughly 200 miles from the First Carrier Strike Force, readying to send off scout planes.

Midway has already launched its PBYs to fly down the spokes of the search route. Every other flyable aircraft is standing by. Once the enemy carriers are spotted, all bombers in every possible combination will strike at the Japanese. Most of the fighters will stay near Midway to tangle with incoming raiders.

The sun will rise at 4:57 A.M., but very few people will be asleep on Sand and Eastern, or on the warships, friendly and enemy, converging on Midway. The pilots and crews have been up for several hours and are ready for action. So are the admirals. Nagumo's mood has changed. He's almost cheerful this morning. He seems positive and optimistic. Already he's said, "The enemy is unaware of our presence in this area and will so remain until our initial attacks on the island." Had Nimitz heard that remark, he would have breathed a bountiful sigh of relief. *He* has achieved surprise.

At 4:25 the *Akagi*'s loudspeakers bark, "All hands to launching stations." Suddenly, the remaining darkness is chased by brilliant floodlights. One "hand" who won't be going to launching stations, however, is Lieutenant Commander Fuchida, the Pearl Harbor leader, now recovering from an emergency appendectomy. He stands forlornly in a hospital robe watching the takeoff proceedings.

The Air Officer leans over the bridge rail to swing his green lamp in an arc, and the Launch Officer, standing in front of the first Zero, beckons it off. Picking up speed, the trim fighter rises into the air, dips slightly, then stabilizes. Eight other Zeros quickly follow.

This dawn pageantry is much the same aboard the *Hiryu, Soryu* and *Kaga,* and within twenty minutes the four carriers have launched 108 aircraft. The planes buzz overhead, collecting, then turn to the southeast toward a pale gold horizon.

Ninety-three planes armed with armor-piercing bombs are held in reserve by Admiral Nagumo to hit American ships, in the remote possibility that any might be around.

Aboard the *Yorktown* at precisely the same time as the *Akagi*'s launch, Admiral Fletcher sends off ten Dauntless dive bombers, ordering them to search one hundred miles in a northern semicircle, west to east. At this moment, and unhappily for Task Forces 16 and 17, the weather is perfect. Visibility in the growing light is thirty-five to forty miles, seas calm with four knots of wind. There is little reason to rejoice over the beauty of the morning. Fletcher and

Spruance would rather be tucked under scattered, gray clouds as Nagumo is.

The bridge clocks tick away. Thirty minutes. Forty minutes. Suspense mounts. Down in the radio rooms ears concentrate on the one set that is tuned to the exact frequency over which the Midway PBYs will report. That set will most likely be the first to bring word of the enemy carrier positions.

Suddenly the voice of Catalina pilot Lieutenant Howard Ady breaks through, "Enemy aircraft." Threading through light squalls, he's spotted a Japanese seaplane coming up fast out of the west. It is obviously a search plane. The enemy pilot holds to his course, ignoring the Catalina. Ady stays on his own course. The little seaplane is a sure sign that the enemy is near.

Ady has had the "choice" search run today just as Ensign Reid had it yesterday, having drawn the long straw that awarded him 315 degrees. Ed Layton had predicted 325 degrees as the approach bearing of the enemy carriers. Flying out 322 degrees, adding more area to his designated search leg on a hunch, Ady will be close enough to Layton's prediction.

Ady continues to chug along in his PBY for another twenty minutes and is amply rewarded. Two Japanese carriers loom up ahead, a bit to starboard. Trying to contain his excitement, Ady radios an electrifying message, *"Enemy carriers!"*

The "flag plots" or admiral's plotting rooms of the American carriers quickly pinpoint the probable position of the enemy. They wait for an additional message from Ady. The teletype machines in the ready rooms chatter out Ady's message on the three-by-three-foot screen: E-N-E-M-Y C-A-R-R-I-E-R-S . . . The pilots sit up.

A few minutes later another Catalina from Midway, flying behind and to the south of Ady, reports to Fletcher, "Many planes heading Midway, bearing 320 degrees, distance 150 miles." Fletcher and Spruance now know that the enemy has launched.

The best time to hit Nagumo will be when he is re-fueling and rearming his returned aircraft. Gas lines will be open; bombs and torpedos will be on deck instead of in the magazines. It is always a critical and highly dangerous time in carrier operations.

Lieutenant Ady continues to stalk the Japanese carriers, skipping in and out of the straggly clouds. A few minutes before 6 A.M., he pins it all down: *"Two carriers and main body of ships, carriers in front, course 135 degrees, speed 25."* Soon Admiral Nimitz goes to CINCPAC Operations Plot, where the two forces have been positioned with the orange and blue markers. The battle will be followed by radio. Nimitz will stay here most of the day.

Commander Layton is jubilant. His remarkable projection of the course of the enemy is only off by five miles. Intelligence has once again provided the fighting men with the edge for victory. It is already an incredible victory for intelligence.

A few minutes after six Admiral Fletcher, knowing that the *Yorktown* must recover her dawn flight of ten search planes before engaging Nagumo, orders Admiral Spruance to take the *Hornet* and the *Enterprise* and "proceed southwesterly and attack enemy carriers when located." In turn, Spruance orders 25 knots for Task Force 16, and the flattops swing around toward the Japanese air fleet. Ready rooms advise pilots that Task Force 16 is on the way. At last there are shouts of approval. Fletcher will follow in the *Yorktown* just as soon as Wally Short's scout planes can be brought back aboard. They are hurrying "home"—that welcoming flight deck with its arrester cables and helping hands.

Air combat is a certainty today. All air groups, and squadrons, are certain to see action, and each type of plane has a specific role to play.

Fighter pilots in teams of two use tactics that are

both offensive and defensive, but with the emphasis on defense—providing the CAP over the task force, escorting the bomber and torpedo planes on their missions and opposing enemy fighters over target.

Maneuvers used in a wild dogfight might appear haphazard with planes zooming all over the sky. But, in fact, they can be likened to ballet, the result of precision training.

The carrier's dive bomber pilots are primarily concerned with cornering and hitting rapidly moving targets. Their aircraft are capable of sustaining a high angle dive—sixty to ninety degrees—braked by wing dive flaps to maintain a constant speed during the latter crucial stages of the attack and the bomb drop. After making allowances for target motion, wind and dive angle, the bomb is dropped at a comparatively low altitude.

Glide bombing, at attack angles of thirty to fifty-five degrees is also used. This is not as difficult as dive bombing, but the aircraft and pilot casualty rates are higher. The approach is high speed, and after release of the bomb, the pilot uses the built-up speed of the "glide" for a quick getaway. Dive brakes or the flaps are not used.

The carrier's torpedo planes are the heavyweights, carrying long, slim torpedoes in their bellies for use against major ships. The "tinfish" attacks, the most dangerous of all, should be coordinated with bombing or strafing attacks to draw away enemy fire and fighter planes. Attacking at slow speeds, coming in low and level and launching at a 1000 yards or less, the torpedo planes are comparatively easy targets for shipboard gunners.

14. Attack On Midway

Sirens howl on Sand and Eastern Islands shortly before 6 A.M., two minutes after Midway's radar picks up the first gang of Japanese "bogeys" ninety-three miles out. They will be met with what is available on Eastern's runway, the old Buffaloes and Wildcats that make up the fighter contingent for the island. Today the emphasis is on attack rather than defense. Nimitz is willing to accept heavy damage to Midway's installations and loss of the fighter aircraft, if the island's planes can get a crack at Nagumo's carriers.

Aloft since dawn and orbiting over a reef fifty miles away, the Army Air Force B-17s have already changed course to pursue the enemy ships. The six new Avengers from the *Hornet,* each packing a torpedo, are also on the way. Then the Army Air Force B-26s, also carrying "tinfish," leave Eastern, followed by sixteen Dauntless dive bombers and eleven Chance-Vought Vindicators (Marine aircraft). More than sixty strike planes from Midway are now heading for Nagumo's carriers.

By 6:20, when the Japanese planes are less than thirty miles away, there are only two aircraft left on the ground at Eastern, both grounded for engine trouble. Their loss will not be significant. Yamamoto's planners had hoped to catch dozens of planes on the ground in this surprise raid.

From the air Midway looks practically deserted. Few men can be seen. The PT boat squadron is cruising around the lagoon as are other boats and launches, making them difficult targets from the air. Each boat bristles with guns, including rifles—anything that can be shot will be used against the Japanese.

The dogfights occurring twenty-five miles off Midway and moving toward shore are not much less than slaughter. The pitiful old Brewster Buffaloes have no chance against the fast Zeros; even the newer Wildcats have trouble coping with the Japanese fighters. American planes are downed every few seconds. In a period of three minutes the Japanese lose three aircraft, but the main strike force is intact as Lieutenant Joichi Tomonaga, air group commander of the *Hiryu*, substituting for the ailing Commander Fuchida, brings them over Midway at 6:31 A.M. only to be greeted by heavy and accurate antiaircraft fire.

Pilots from the *Kaga* and *Hiryu* go after the hangar, fuel storage tanks and seaplane ramps of Sand; *Akagi* and *Soryu* fliers take care of Eastern's powerhouse, mess hall and command post. Midway seems to leap out of the water as bombs are stepped across the lagoon in thundering red and black blotches. Sand's fuel tanks explode and oily smoke covers the atoll. Fighters scream down through it, strafing and firing at any target.

The raid lasts less than twenty minutes. The Japanese are now winging away. Their losses have been comparatively light—six aircraft destroyed, fifteen or so damaged. Midway is writhing in smoke and flames. But, suddenly, quiet descends, except for the crackle of flames. The guns are still, the booming has stopped. With all the noise suddenly ended, the sound of voices is a relief.

At 7:15, Captain Simard orders an "all clear." He believes the Japanese will return, but he may have an hour or so to reload guns, put out fires, tend to the wounded and prepare for a second wave. Soon six of the Marine fighter planes, each one shot up, stagger in. Only six.

A calamity has struck Marine Squadron 221. Out of twenty-five pilots only ten are alive. Four of them had parachuted to safety. Only two of the aircraft now landing will ever fly again. VMF-221 has been wiped out, the largest single Marine air loss of World War II. The surviving pilots are bitter. Those Brewster Buffaloes *were* flying coffins.

During the next hour, Captain Simard and Colonel Shannon survey the damage. Fuel storage gone, mess hall gone, dispensary destroyed, power plant blown up, hangar gone, and seaplane ramps destroyed. Of the ground personnel eleven are dead, seventeen wounded. The antiaircraft batteries are still intact, and the aircraft runways on Eastern are okay. Midway can fight back from the ground, though not from the air.

15. Pilots, Man Your Planes

Thinking of the long distance the pilots will have to travel to hit the enemy and then return, Admiral Spruance had planned to launch the aircraft of Task Force 16 at 9 A.M., when Nagumo's carriers would be less than a hundred miles away. But crusty, brawling Captain Miles Browning, his chief of staff inherited from "Bull" Halsey, finally persuades him to order a takeoff at 7 A.M. Browning is an experienced aviator and understands the risks of pilots running out of fuel. He admits that some will probably have to ditch in the ocean. Nonetheless, he believes that the U.S. must strike the first blow and do it now at the maximum fuel range of the Wildcats and Devastators. Spruance finally agrees.

Then loudspeakers in the *Hornet* and *Enterprise* rasp out, "Pilots, man your planes." The fliers hope that this time the call to action is for real. The two previous false starts this morning haven't helped their nerves. Briefings in each ready room are finished. The pilots have scribbled down up-to-date information on the enemy's position, course, speed, probable location from hour to hour, weather data, and very importantly, the home carrier's *point option*—where the flattop is supposed to be upon their return from target.

Togged out in flight and safety gear—yellow "Mae West" lifejackets (inflatable rubber vests), goggles perched on their foreheads, gloves, parachute harnesses slapping their backs—they pound up the lad-

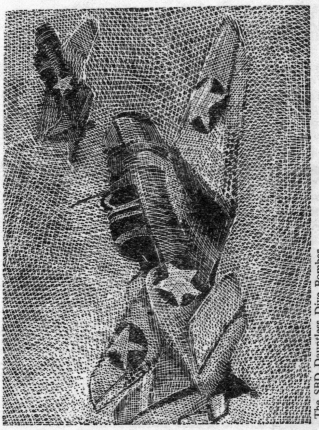

The SBD Dauntless Dive Bomber

ders to the flight deck, clutching flight charts. Pilots have right of way on these ladders, even admirals must step aside. Once again, the drama and pageantry of flight operations begins with propellers turning on deck.

Torpedo 8's Jack Waldron goes up to the bridge of the *Hornet* to say a few words to Captain Marc "Pete" Mitscher. He tells Mitscher he'll take his planes in and get hits. Mitscher has already read the message Waldron handed out to his squadron: *If there is only one plane left to make a final run. . . .* The captain of the *Hornet* does not answer, but leans out of his high bridge chair and touches the slender, fierce pilot on the shoulder. Then Waldron goes aft on the flight deck past the dive bombers, and climbs into his heavy-bellied aircraft. The white-nosed torpedo is tucked away inside.

The *Hornet*'s Wildcat fighters are already streaking up into the air at 7:05 A.M. Next off are the Dauntlesses of Scouting 5, loaded as bombers this morning. Bombing 5 then answers the white flag. Waldron's "pickle planes," as he calls them, are off last.

The gunners of the dive bombers and torpedo planes, facing to the rear in order to spot enemy aircraft and fire the twin .30 calibre machine-guns, are the last to see the carriers after takeoff. The gunners get a panoramic view of the busy flight decks as the planes roar away. With the gunners guarding to the rear and above, firing at attacking enemy fighter planes, the pilots handle targets ahead of the aircraft, firing fixed guns. For the pilot to fire these guns, the aircraft must be aimed at the target.

Air group commander for the *Enterprise* is Wade McClusky, a very impatient aviator who is now circling Task Force 16 at 20,000 feet, sucking on oxygen, and waiting for all the "Big E's" fighters, dive bombers and torpedo planes to be launched. It is taking an abnormally long time. Spruance, after agreeing with Miles Browning's wisdom for an early strike, decided to throw every available aircraft at Nagumo, except for a few Wildcats retained as CAP. Only a half-deck load can go off at one launching to allow enough flight deck length for takeoff. The other half is then brought up on the elevators from the hangar deck and spotted.

While McClusky orbits, the Japanese planes that just attacked Midway are heading back toward the First Carrier Striking Force. Their leader, Lieutenant Tomonaga, radios to Nagumo, asking for another bombing run at the island. He had circled Sand and Eastern before departing, saw fires burning and other evidence of heavy damage, but also observed that Eastern's runways were still in good shape. The Americans could fly in dozens of aircraft and operate them from Eastern before the Japanese invasion troops splashed ashore. However, this message is not taken kindly on the flag bridge of the *Akagi*. Admiral Nagumo had no plans for another raid on Midway. Moreover, he has ninety-three planes spotted on his carrier decks all armed to deal specifically with enemy ships, not shore installations. They carry armor-piercing bombs and torpedoes, not the instant-contact explosives used for land attacks. "Breaking the spot" —sending all the aircraft below to rearm them with instant-contact weapons—will take the better part of an hour. During that time the aircraft will be useless, unavailable for any type of mission.

Nagumo, a man set in his ways, begins to debate the problem with his staff. They point out to him that search planes from the cruisers have not detected any American ships in the area, though one reconnaisance seaplane from the cruiser *Tone* has not as yet completed its sector search. In addition to the welcome silence from the search planes, Tokyo hasn't sent word of any radio intercepts from ships in the Central Pacific. The Combined Fleet submarines, supposedly off Hawaii this morning, haven't warned of the departure of major fleet units. So it is concluded that no U.S. ships are in the area, exactly as Nagumo had said earlier.

The debate lasts less than five minutes because air raid alarms are ringing on the vessels of the Japanese First Carrier Force. Pesky planes from Midway, the six new Grumman Avengers carrying torpedos, are making their battle debut, riding into the very heart of the enemy task force without fighter escort.

Boring in behind the Avengers are the four Army B-26 bombers, carrying weapons the Army never uses —torpedoes. The Army pilots have had no training in hitting ships. There is only one tactical plan, *sink the carriers*. But how to sink them is another matter.

Chased by skilled Zero pilots into a wall of antiaircraft fire, five planes are shot down before they reach position to launch their torpedoes. Four planes reach launching position, but are shot down by ack-ack fire, one crashing onto the *Akagi* and skidding into the sea. Of the six Avengers from the temporary land unit of the *Hornet,* only one survives; of the four B-26s, two limp back to Midway heavily shot up.

However, Nagumo and his staff are shaken. No one had expected such ferocious, courageous, perhaps even foolhardy opposition from the Americans. Until this moment, Nagumo and his key officers had questioned the "fighting spirit" of the Americans. Now there is no longer any question about sending a second strike to Midway. Those torpedo planes obviously came from that strip at Eastern and more will come unless bombs wreck it.

Nagumo immediately orders the ninety-three aircraft—those reserved especially to hit the American carriers—to be sent below. The torpedo planes will be rearmed with bombs for land targets; the bombers will substitute their armor-piercing variety for instant-contact explosives. The work involves unstrapping the torpedoes, each one weighing more than a thousand pounds, taking them to the racks, trundling the replacement bombs out of magazines and strapping them on. It will take the Japanese sailors at least an hour to make the changes.

Six hundred miles away, steaming northeast of

Midway with his giant battleships, Admiral Yamamoto receives word that the first strike on the island base has been completed and a second strike is necessary. All seems to be going well. The admiral has recovered from his stomach ailment and is in exceptionally good humor this morning. He and his staff are clad in their white dress uniforms. Yamamoto isn't particularly bothered by the fact that the enemy has discovered Nagumo's carriers and has sent land-based aircraft from Midway to attack. This was to be expected, the admiral says. Nagumo has plenty of fighter aircraft and his ships have tremendous antiaircraft power.

Thirteen minutes after Yamamoto expresses confidence in his carriers, Admiral Nagumo receives the first of a series of jolts. Search plane No. 4 from the cruiser *Tone*, the last seaplane launched, reports, *"Ten ships, apparently enemy, sighted. Bearing 010. Distance 240 miles from Midway. Course 150. Speed more than 20 knots. Time 0728."*

There is an awful, stunned silence on the *Akagi* flag bridge. The Americans were not supposed to arrive until *after* Midway was invaded. There has been absolutely no indication from any Japanese intelligence source—anywhere—that any U.S. ships were in the Midway area. This is not the way it was planned in the war games at Hashirajima anchorage.

The position of the "apparent" enemy is quickly plotted at 200 miles, just within striking range of the Zeros, Vals and Kates. But Nagumo is also very much aware that his own ships are now within range of the Wildcats, Dauntlesses and Devastators. He wonders if there is a carrier in that group of ships and has it launched aircraft?

Nagumo is in a terrible quandary. He's already begun rearming for the strike on Midway. Should he now stop that work and order the rearming of the torpedoes and armor-piercing bombs? Hits with the land-type bombs can seldom severely cripple or sink warships. More debate consumes the next fifteen precious minutes. Finally, Nagumo signals his carriers, "Prepare to carry out attacks against enemy fleet units. Leave torpedoes on those planes which have not yet changed to land bombs." But many have already changed, and another time-consuming change will be necessary.

Then the thoroughly rattled Nagumo messages the *Tone* pilot, "Ascertain ship types and maintain contact."

Two minutes later the seaplane pilot informs the admiral that the enemy has changed course, but doesn't mention ship types. The enraged Nagumo whips a message right back, demanding to know if the enemy has a carrier.

As soon as this searing communiqué leaves the *Akagi* sixteen Marine dive bombers from Midway begin their high-speed glide bomb runs. Nagumo's CAP of Zeros is there, and eight of the Dauntlesses are shot down.

By the time the surviving Marine bombers are chased off, the *Tone* pilot answers Nagumo's last request, "Enemy ships are five cruisers and five destroyers."

Despite the fact that Army Air Force B-17s from Midway are now attacking, sending up huge geysers of water around the swerving ships as their bombs explode, there is vast relief on the *Akagi* flag bridge. There is back-slapping, laughter and wide smiles, including a grin on the face of the sour Nagumo.

"Just as I thought, there are no carriers," says Nagumo's staff intelligence officer, Lieutenant Commander Ono. They are confident that five cruisers and five destroyers can be handled quite easily. As of 8:15 A.M. on this warm June day, the atmosphere on the flag bridge of the *Akagi* is once again relaxed, even cheerful.

So far the Japanese carriers have been attacked by sixty enemy planes, all from Midway, and not one ship has been put out of action. Not even a "near miss"—a bomb that does not hit its target, but falls close enough to cause damage—has scored. The Americans have yet to do more than shake a ship.

However, the admiral and his staff are only able to enjoy the relaxed atmosphere and good cheer for five minutes. At 8:20 the *Tone* pilot transmits another message, which appalls Nagumo and his officers. *"The enemy is accompanied by what appears to be a carrier."*

The *Yorktown* and her escorts have been sighted. The *Tone* pilot fails to spot the *Hornet* and the *Enterprise*. They aren't far away, and aircraft launching on both is almost completed.

16. Does Yamamoto Have "Victory Fever"?

Though the American planes from Midway have made no hits after an hour of attack, they've kept the Japanese First Carrier Force in constant turmoil, zig-zagging to dodge bombs and torpedoes, the Japanese gunners on edge. An anxious destroyer screening the *Kaga* has just mistakenly fired on Lieutenant Tomonaga's air group, returning from the Midway bombing run. A "cease fire" is hastily ordered and Tomonaga's planes, some full of holes, begin to touch down at 8:37 A.M.

The work of changing bombs to torpedoes continues at a furious pace while the returning aircraft are landed and sent below. There isn't time to store the land-type bombs properly, so they are simply stacked like cordwood on the hangar decks, a potentially lethal situation on any carrier.

Another disturbing element has been added to the American attack. The U.S. submarine *Nautilus* has stealthily joined the fight, sending a torpedo at one of the escorting Japanese battleships. Though it missed, the underwater scare is enough to bring the destroyer *Arashi* to the scene. She stays over the submarine position, dumping depth charges.

With the Midway strike plane recovery due to be completed around 9:00 A.M., Nagumo sends a blinker message to all his ships, "After completing recovery operations, Force will temporarily head northward. We plan to contact and destroy enemy." Next he radios Admiral Yamamoto, informing him of the presence of a U.S. carrier.

The news is greeted with great enthusiasm on the admiral's "bridge" of the *Yamato*. This is the exact message that the Japanese commander in chief has been waiting and hoping for. It is the main reason *Operation MI* was devised in the first place—to draw out the American fleet and sink it.

But no one stops to answer two important questions: How did this enemy force get so close without any intelligence warning? And are there other American carriers lurking nearby? Yamamoto, who was so worried about "victory fever" earlier, now seems to have caught it himself. He doesn't seem to be concerned about the Yankee flattop.

A few minutes after sending the communiqué to Yamamoto, Admiral Nagumo changes course northward and again confidently signals his force, "The first strikes will be launched at 10:30."

Rear Admiral Tamon Yamaguchi, commander of Carrier Division Two and the brilliant, aggressive officer thought to be in line to succeed Yamamoto someday, flashes a message from his flagship *Hiryu,* "Consider it advisable to launch attack force immediately." Yamaguchi is very much concerned about that elusive "single" American carrier. He wants to launch what is available with whatever bombs and torpedoes are already loaded right now. Forget about the fighter escort, if necessary, just bomb that enemy carrier before it is too late!

But Commander Genda has already talked to Nagumo, advising that it is better to wait. He reasons that they'll have enough time to send all the planes with their proper bomb loads. Genda has another concern. He knows nearly every pilot in the fleet and doesn't want to send them out without fighter escort.

Nagumo, as usual, listens to Commander Genda's advice and replies to Yamaguchi negatively. The admiral is still convinced that he can strike the first blow. As the sun mounts ever higher, there is some reason to believe that he may be right. The time is 9:15 A.M.

17. Torpedo Planes Slaughtered

What is about to occur here off Midway Island on June 4, 1942, becomes the finest single chapter in American naval history. No other event shines so brightly. The names of the individual pilots faded long ago, but their deeds—many of which are sacrificial without meaning to be—live on. It is incredible, furthermore, because it was mostly born of mistakes.

There is no real coordination between the attacking planes of the *Hornet, Enterprise* and *Yorktown,* which launched last. They are simply all heading for a common target, the Japanese carrier fleet. Admiral Spruance had hoped for a coordinated attack, but the length of time needed to launch one, the limited experience of the pilots and the inexperience of American carrier warfare itself rule out much in the way of coordination.

Already there are foul-ups. Commander Max Leslie, leading the *Yorktown's* Bombing 3, has no bomb. Neither do three of his pilots. The bombs fell off the aircrafts because of mechanical malfunctions. So they're roaring toward the mighty Japanese carriers armed only with machine gun bullets.

The *Hornet's* air group commander, Stanhope Ring, is leading his dive bombers, scouts and fighters on a wild goose chase *away* from the enemy. Ring steered his aircraft in the wrong direction.

And Jim Gray, assigned to protect the *Enterprise*

torpedo planes with his Wildcat fighters, is following the wrong group—Waldron's *Hornet* torpedo squadron, which has split away from the other *Hornet* planes.

The "Big E's" torpedo aircraft, commanded by Gene Lindsey, have no protection. The torpedomen are doomed.

Before takeoff from the *Hornet*, Jack Waldron had told one of his pilots, Ensign George Gay, "I believe the Japs will change course. Just keep on my tail, and I'll lead you to them . . ." At about 9:20 A.M. Waldron does lead Torpedo 8 straight to the enemy—and to death. He sights the First Carrier Force on the horizon and alters his course, waggling his wings to signal, "Follow me." Apparently he believed that Stanhope Ring's *Hornet* fighters were above him to help in the attack. But by now even Jim Gray and his *Enterprise* fighters have lost track of the planes below. Waldron and his heavy-bellied planes are alone in the thick of the Japanese fleet.

Nagumo has his carriers in a box formation with the two battleships, three cruisers and eleven destroyers ringing them for antiaircraft concentration. The *Akagi* is to the right, astern of her is the *Kaga*. To the left is the *Hiryu*, astern of her is the *Soryu*.

Waldron begins heading for the *Soryu* in the rear of the column. Even at this distance of three or four miles he begins to get antiaircraft bursts from the escorts. He adjusts the throttle and drops lower. The squadron follows him down. Zeros hurtle by, guns firing, but there is no one to help Jack Waldron and his "pickle planes." The *Hornet* fighters are far to the southwest. Jim Gray's "Big E" fighters are up in the clouds, waiting to be summoned. Torpedo 8 will have to go it alone.

Off to left a plane explodes in flames. Waldron asks who it belongs to? Ensign Gay replies, "One of ours."

As Waldron continues to lead the run-in before the

torpedo drop, he pleads in vain on the radio for Stan Ring to help. "Stanhope from Johnny One, answer, answer . . ."

Waldron shouts, "Watch those fighters . . . see that splash? How'm I doin', Dobbs?" Dobbs is Waldron's rear gunner. Waldron's plane is suddenly awash in flames. Ensign Gay sees him standing fully erect in the cockpit just before the Devastator cartwheels into the sea.

One plane after another bursts into flame, then dives or veers sideways into the ocean. Not one torpedo hit has been made. Torpedo 8 is being wiped out.

By 9:28, three of Waldron's "pickle plane" survivors are still boring in on the *Soryu*. Then, suddenly, there is only one plane left—piloted by Ensign George Gay. He feels his aircraft thump from the impact of bullets. He also feels a sharp pain in his arm. Then there is silence from his gunner. He looks back. The gunner is dead, hanging from his straps, slumped over the machine gun.

Miraculously the aircraft is still strumming along in the middle of ack-ack bursts. Gay drives it around the big carrier while squeezing the bullet from his arm. He clenches it in his teeth for safe-keeping.

He releases his torpedo at a distance of about 800 yards, then flies right along the deck of the *Soryu* close enough to see faces on the bridge. Dropping the Devastator lower as he clears the stern of the carrier, Gay is immediately overwhelmed by Zeros. His controls are shot out. He must make a hard landing in the ocean, but still manages to escape from the plane. Gay inflates his "Mae West" lifejacket, and recovers the liferaft. He then ducks under a cushion from the plane to hide from the shipboard machine gunners of the escorts. From that unusual vantage point, George Gay, the only survivor of the *Hornet*'s Torpedo 8, watches the Battle Off Midway Island.

Gene Lindsey is now bringing his Torpedo 6 from the "Big E" in toward the enemy carriers and is wondering what happened to Jim Gray and his fighter escort. Back on the *Enterprise* they'd worked it all out. Lindsey was to radio, "Hey, Jim, come on down," when he needed help. Well, he'll be needing it very soon, and Jim isn't answering. Gray, still up in those high clouds, hears nothing.

At 9:30, Lindsey gears up Torpedo 6 for a strike on the *Kaga* and his fourteen "tinfish" planes spear toward the carrier with just a few miles to go. He is still broadcasting, "Jim, come down, come on down . . ."

The Nagumo force is no longer in a neat box formation. The attacks have spread the ships and the *Hiryu* is well ahead, on the horizon.

As Lindsey begins his final run at the *Kaga*, the Zeros of CAP descend. It is a quick, vicious replay of the Torpedo 8 destruction. Within twenty minutes, ten of the fourteen planes, including Lindsey's, have been blown out of the sky. Not much has gone right since Howard Ady first reported spotting Nagumo at 5:52 A.M. Combined with the aircraft casualties from Midway, the toll has become frightening.

Nagumo has one more group of visitors on the way —Lieutenant Commander Lance E. Massey's twelve Devastators from the *Yorktown*. For a welcome change, Massey is escorted by Fighting 3, or part of it, consisting of six Wildcats led by Jimmy Thach, probably the best fighter pilot in the Navy.

Flashing by with guns stuttering, the superb Zeros come homing in when Massey has his *Yorktowners* about fifteen or sixteen miles from the Japanese carriers. Rear-seat gunners return the fire with their flexible .30 calibre machine guns. The Zeros don't score on this pass. They roar up and around for another run as Massey drops the squadron to 150 feet.

Passing through the outer screen of Japanese destroyers, ack-ack aids the buzzing Zeros as Massey keeps grimly on his course toward the "outboard carrier," probably the *Kaga*. At least eight enemy fighters are swirling the air around Torpedo 3, and Massey's call for help to Jimmy Thach, now a thousand feet above, can't be answered. Thach's six Wildcats are dogfighting with more than a dozen Zeros. The first flaming casualty of Torpedo 3 dives for the ocean.

18. The Battle Turns

At 10:20 A.M., Admiral Nagumo is about five minutes away from being able to launch his strike at the American "carrier," the apparent source of all these nuisance attacks by torpedo planes. His own torpedo-carrying Kates and Val dive bombers are warming up on the flight decks, spotted behind the Zeros.

Gas lines are open on all the Japanese carriers. The instant-contact bombs, which were to be used on the runways at Eastern, have not yet been stowed safely in the magazines. There hasn't been enough time to do that job. The last lanes are still being re-armed at this moment. The captains of all four flattops are very much aware of the dangers of the exposed bombs and open fuel lines should the enemy attack. The usual safety procedures have been completely disregarded in an effort to quickly launch the new strike.

The *Akagi, Kaga* and *Soryu* are now steaming in a loose formation, the *Kaga* in the middle and astern. Their wakes make long, churning trails in the ocean. The *Hiryu* is a considerable distance ahead, to the north and out of sight. Nagumo gives orders to "launch when ready," even though the *Yorktown* planes are still attacking.

Almost simultaneously, Lance Massey's plane is hit. He climbs out onto the burning wing as the aircraft plunges into the sea. Ten of Torpedo 3's planes have gone down, and no hits have been made.

Out of forty-one torpedo planes from the three squadrons of the *Hornet,* the *Enterprise* and the *Yorktown,* thirty-five have been destroyed with a tragic loss of pilots and gunners, the most concentrated naval aviation loss of World War II. However, their brave attacks have not been in vain. They've forced the carriers to twist and turn, preventing the launching of aircraft. More importantly, they've also drawn the Japanese CAP down to low altitudes and off station. The CAP must now climb back up to station to fight off dive bombers should they attack. The climb to twelve or fifteen thousand feet will take at least four or five minutes.

The *Akagi* begins her turn into the wind, props spinning on her flight deck. Within a minute, the *Kaga* and *Soryu* will begin sending planes up to attack the *Yorktown.* Undoubtedly, they'll also find the "Big E" and *Hornet.*

However, as if he'd actually heard the chunky admiral order the launching on the Japanese carriers, Lieutenant Commander Max Leslie initiates his own brand of action at about 14,500 feet, diving out of fluffy clouds. The sixteen planes of *Yorktown's* Bombing 3 follow him, forming an arrow.

There isn't a Zero in sight. The Japanese fighters are still angling upward, trying to get back on CAP station. Antiaircraft gunners on the ships are searching for torpedo plane targets, not attacks from overhead. They aren't looking up. For several minutes, Nagumo's ships put up no defense at all.

The nose of Leslie's Dauntless is almost pointed straight down at the big red "meatball" on the yellow carrier deck. He holds the quivering plane on target, driving down at 270 mph at an angle of 70 degrees. Lacking a bomb, he can only punish the enemy by strafing. He pushes his button, watching the tracer bullets fall away toward the carrier like red rain. At

4,000 feet his guns jam. Leslie then pulls out of the dive, having led his squadron to target.

The plane behind Leslie's is piloted by Ensign Paul "Swede" Holmberg. As Leslie clears, "Swede" Holmberg rides down to 2,500 feet and releases his bomb both manually and electrically, making certain it will fall. As Holmberg lifts the screaming Dauntless up again, he turns slightly to view the results. *A clean hit!*

Fire and black smoke rise from the carrier deck. An enemy aircraft is thrown overboard like a toy.

The other planes of Bombing 3 are driving down, one after the other, toward Holmberg's vacant pull-out spot. Other bombs tumble, and when the run is over, four out of eight have found a fiery home.

Of course, no one in Bombing 3 knows the name of this carrier, and for the moment it doesn't really matter. It is simply a big target with a fifty-foot red "meat-ball" on it, very likely a veteran of the Pearl Harbor raid.

For years after this midmorning fireworks display on the Pacific, pilots of the *Enterprise* and the *Yorktown* will argue over who "got" the *Kaga* or the *Soryu*. The *Yorktown* men will swear they nailed the *Kaga*. "Big E" men will heatedly maintain that it was the *Soryu* that the *Yorktown* bombed. The *Kaga* was all theirs, they will say. Such was the confusion of the attack.

But whichever Japanese flattop felt the wrath of Bombing 3, it is now reeling with explosions. The flight deck is peeled back in places with jagged sections of steel jutting out like an opened can. The deck is already red hot in places. There are men running around the ship in flames. Pilots awaiting takeoff have been cremated at their controls. Gasoline-fed fires are raging. Bombs are exploding. Men jump into the sea without waiting for orders to abandon ship.

Max Leslie's men, having performed brilliantly, head back for the *Yorktown*, knowing that Zeros from the CAP will probably make passes at them. Thanks to the earlier torpedo attacks that drew away the enemy fighters, all of Bombing 3 has survived.

Before Leslie's runs are even finished, other dive bombers are hurtling down on the other two carriers. *Enterprise* planes attack in what appears to be an intricately coordinated plan with the *Yorktown* strike force. It is the kind of perfect textbook situation that would please instructors at the Naval War College—*Yorktown* planes concentrating on one carrier while the larger *Enterprise* group hits the other flattops simultaneously. But, in fact, the timing of the two strikes, with Leslie coming in from one angle and Wade McClusky coming from another, is pure luck.

Luck has played a great part in the *Enterprise* planes even finding Nagumo's task force. At 9:50, McClusky was leading his thirty-three dive bombers of the "Big E's" Bombing 6 and Scouting 6 on the course provided for him by Air Plot. From 19,000 feet he'd seen nothing but empty ocean below. Worse yet, he was nearing the point where he'd have to turn the planes back because of fuel limitations. Then he spotted a knife of white water laid over the blue ocean and took a closer look with binoculars. He guessed that it was a destroyer, running at full speed and "throwing white water," and further gambled that it was headed for Nagumo country. He turned to her course.

The gamble paid off handsomely. The destroyer was the *Arashi*, left behind by the other escorts to deal with the submarine *Nautilus* at about 8 A.M. She was steaming full ahead to catch up with the carriers. Soon McClusky saw the wakes of many other ships ahead. It was Nagumo country all right.

Now, at 10:21, McClusky is above the carriers, and all three are apparently readying to launch aircraft. No better time to attack, for simultaneously Leslie is diving with his *Yorktown* planes. McClusky chooses the carrier on the right for himself and Earl Gallaher's

Scouting 6. He radios to Dick Best, who is leading
Bombing 6, ". . . you take the one on the left."

These words begin the tearing out of the heart of
the Japanese fleet. In a matter of 120 seconds between
10:24 and 10:26 A.M., June 4, 1942, the entire course
of the Pacific war begins to be reversed.

At about 10:24, the Air Officer of the *Akagi* whips
his white flag down, signaling the first spotted plane to
take off. Just as the Zero starts to roll, a lookout yells,
"Hell divers," pointing upward to the Wildcats that
are arrowing down. A second Zero speeds off. These
are the last two planes ever to operate from the flagship *Akagi*.

The leader of the Pearl Harbor raid, Lieutenant
Commander Fuchida, is still out on deck in his bath-
robe, observing flight operations. He looks up to see
enemy planes diving straight down on the *Akagi*. Antiaircraft guns open fire, but it is too late. Fuchida runs
for cover.

Dick Best's Bombing 6 planes take the carrier on
the right, not the left as McClusky had assigned. They
are now strung out in a line. From three of the planes
float down "dark objects"—thousand-pound bombs.
Fuchida stares at them, entranced. The first one, provided by Lieutenant Best, is a near miss, exploding op-
posite the bridge island. The second one penetrates to
the hangar and detonates loose bombs, literally lifting
the *Akagi* out of the water from concussion, or so it
seemed. The third bomb hits in the very center of all
the planes spotted on the flight deck. They are loaded
with gasoline, bombs and torpedos. Pieces of planes
fly through the air for hundreds of feet. Human bodies
disintegrate. Burning gas cascades in all directions.
The flight deck is an instant inferno.

Fuchida, horrified at the destruction that had been
wrought in a matter of seconds, staggers down a ladder
and into a ready room. He passes men who were
charred at their posts.

Within five minutes, the once proud *Akagi* is completely out of control, communication to her engine room having been destroyed. She is burning fiercely from stem to stern.

The story is much the same on the *Soryu*. She has taken three direct bomb hits and is another inferno. Black smoke coils up a thousand feet above her.

Nagumo's chief of staff, Admiral Kusaka, advises his superior to leave the *Akagi* immediately. At first the admiral refuses to go. He cannot believe that in a period of two minutes he has lost three carriers. Kusaka then reminds him that his duty is to the entire fleet, not just this pyre of a flagship. As commander of the entire task force, he must continue the battle.

Nagumo, totally bewildered and in shock, is finally led to a rope like a child by the hand. He lowers himself to the fiery deck, then is guided to a safer part of the ship where he is transferred to the cruiser *Nagara*.

Time is logged in at 10:46 A.M., just twenty-two minutes after that first near miss exploded.

As Nagumo's flag breaks out from the *Nagara*, the commanding officer of the *Soryu* gives orders to abandon ship. The carrier is a helpless mass of flames. Captain Ryusaku Yanagimoto makes certain that his order is clearly understood, then steps back into the raging fire, seeking *senshi*—battle death.

19. Yamamoto Cannot Speak

Over the horizon the *Hiryu* has not been seen by the raiders of Task Forces 16 and 17. From the bridge Admiral Yamaguchi addresses the pilots, telling them that the other carriers have been attacked and are burning and that it is now "up to the *Hiryu* to carry on the fight for the glory of Japan." Leader of the first eighteen Val dive bombers and six Zeros will be Lieutenant Michio Kobayashi, a veteran of every Nagumo raid from Pearl Harbor to the Indian Ocean.

Yamaguchi also plans a torpedo attack within the hour. But not unexpectedly, the admiral is suffering from an aircraft shortage. A number of the aircraft used for the Midway strike are not operational. In addition to the eighteen Vals, he has a total of twelve Zeros and ten Kate torpedo planes.

At 10:55, Kobayashi's planes rise up from the *Hiryu* and turn east, forming up for the flight to the "single" American carrier. They are led by a pair of seaplanes from a cruiser. The seaplane guides are soon unnecessary as Kobayashi sights a group of American planes headed back for the *Yorktown* and begins following them. However, he quickly loses two of his escorting Zeros. They swoop down on Max Leslie's returning Dauntlesses of Bombing 3 and are promptly shot up by rear-seat gunners.

As this comeuppance is being dealt out with machine gun bullets, another kind of comeuppance is being felt in the floating headquarters of the Combined

Fleet. The *Yamato* and her large brood of battleships is still hundreds of miles from Midway.

Admiral Yamamoto has just read a message from what is left of the First Carrier Forces: *"Fires raging aboard* Kaga, Soryu *and* Akagi *resulting from attacks by enemy carrier and land-based planes. We plan to have the* Hiryu *engage the enemy carrier. We are temporarily withdrawing to the north to assemble our forces."*

Yamamoto and his staff had been expecting word of a great victory from Nagumo. This news is completely shattering, and the bridge of the *Yamato* becomes so "gloomy as to make one ill," according to the admiral's yoeman, Mitsuhara Noda.

After groaning on first reading the text, the commander in chief makes no other sound. He cannot even speak for a few minutes and stands frozen. Outside there is heavy fog, which adds to the feeling of hopelessness. For months, the officers and men of the Imperial Navy have been telling themselves how good they are. The news from the blazing sea off Midway is a great shock. In many ways, it is unbelievable.

Yamamoto finally pulls himself together and begins to make decisions. He will rush immediately to the defeated Task Force with his own Main Body and engage the enemy. He announces to his staff that he'll take personal charge of the battle.

20. Target—*Yorktown*

As noon approaches, the *Yorktown* is a busy ship. She has just received Jimmy Thach's five surviving but shot-up Wildcats and two wobbling planes from the *Enterprise,* one of them cartwheeling in. Landing operations are halted for a few minutes.

Orbiting above are Max Leslie's dive bombers, returning from strikes on Nagumo's carriers. Also up there are twelve Wildcats of the early afternoon CAP shift. Just as word is given to land Leslie's planes, which are low on fuel, the *Yorktown's* radar picks the enemy out of the sky. *"Bogeys coming in from just south of west, distance forty-six miles!"*

If Spruance and Fletcher, lacking sighting reports, had doubts about the existence of a fourth Japanese carrier, the "Yorky's" radar answers their questions. The enemy planes are climbing, indicating dive bombers. Torpedo planes should be coming in low.

The *Yorktown* with all hands on deck now prepares for attack. Gasoline lines are drained, and nonflammable carbon dioxide is pumped into the empty fuel lines. A huge auxiliary tank of high-test aviation gas is pushed over the stern. With luck what occurred in the Japanese carriers won't happen in the *Yorktown.* In Condition Zed—battle condition—she buttons up below decks. Watertight doors are checked and closed. Speed is upped to 30.5 knots, everything she has.

Max Leslie makes his approach to land but is waved off, which baffles him. "Swede" Holmberg fol-

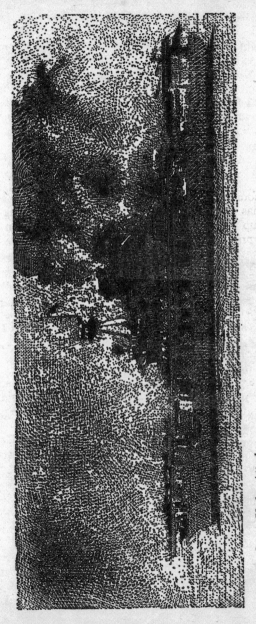

The *Yorktown* Under Attack

lows him down and is not only given a wave-off, but is jolted by explosions as the *Yorktown*'s five-inch guns cut loose at the enemy. The radio shouts angrily at Leslie to take his group elsewhere. "*Yorktown* is under attack."

The squadron commander hustles them away to safety. More orbiting is necessary though gas is critical. Ditching is imminent.

The ship's *fighter-director officer* vectors the orbiting CAP out to meet the *Hiryu* planes. At high noon, fifteen miles from the carrier at 10,000 feet, Kobayashi and his planes in a "vee of vees" are jumped by twelve Wildcats. As the dogfight moves in and out of the clouds, six Japanese planes fall. But Kobayashi presses on, now heading into heavy antiaircraft fire from the escorts and *Yorktown* herself.

Despite CAP's attacks and escort gunnery, eight of the Vals—muddy brown on top, silver on the bottom, with gleaming yellow tails—make it to dive positions over the *Yorktown*. They push down, coming in wide open at 70-degree angles, making them difficult to hit.

Captain Elliott Buckmaster is maneuvering his ship skillfully, but there is no way to avoid the chain of Vals descending on him. The *Yorktown* twists and turns, but seems to be in slow motion. Three near misses lift the ship out of the water, exposing her drumming propellers. She surges on, every available knot of speed being strained from her boilers.

Kobayashi's plane suddenly explodes, and the Val behind him catches fire and veers off. But these losses don't deter the next six aircraft. They maintain rigid dive angles and make their drops. One after the other, the bombs fall almost straight down.

The first explosive hits the flight deck near the base of the *Yorktown*'s island. The second bomb punctures the flight deck and explodes in the uptakes of the ship's firerooms, which is part of the exhaust systems. The fires go out in five boilers. A third bomb goes down the forward flight deck elevator space and explodes in a rag storage room, near ammunition lockers and high-octane gas storages. Rags are used in ship's clean-up work and once afire are difficult to extinguish.

None of the hits are fatal, but ears are still ringing. Damage-control crews are at work within a minute of the blasts. The sprinkler system is showering water on the hangar deck. Carbon dioxide is being pumped into the high-octane storage tanks.

Combustion gases from the shattered uptakes fill the firerooms. The engine gang with gas masks on attempt to keep a pair of burners going under one of the boilers. This move provides just enough steam for the electric generators and the pumps, but not enough to power the engines. At 12:20, the *Yorktown* comes to a stop. Nevertheless there is every indication that she'll make hasty repairs, put the rag fire out, treat her wounded, get underway and fight again.

However, Admiral Fletcher has wasted little time in shifting his flag to the cruiser *Astoria*. He knows he can't wage war in a drifting ship.

At about the same time, Admiral Yamamoto sends a positive message to all his ships. He intends to attack the enemy off Midway, he says. He summons forces from the Aleutians invasion group, ordering them to steam at full speed to the side of the *Hiryu*. He directs Admiral Nobutake Kondo to bring his battleships and cruisers to the carrier's position. He'll add his own Main Body as soon as possible. The Midway troop transports won't be needed until after he defeats the American fleet, so he orders them to retire temporarily.

Yamamoto certainly isn't retreating. He's hopeful that Admiral Kondo can engage Spruance and Fletcher in a night gunnery duel with the assistance of four cruisers of the close support group. Their targets will be Sand and Eastern Islands.

As the afternoon progresses, the *Yorktown,* now dead in the water, has a fire burning deep within her. Three Japanese carriers are blazing. More than a hundred Imperial Navy ships are steaming full speed to assist the *Hiryu.*

On the bridge of the *Hornet,* Captain Mitscher is very uneasy. There's been no word from any of the planes of his Air Group 8. Then twenty minutes later, they begin to flutter in. Air Group Commander Stan Ring tells Mitscher that it has been a frustrating, humiliating morning for the *Hornet.* They didn't find the enemy carriers. Some planes ran out of gas and flopped into the water. Others made it to Midway for refueling.

"Where is Torpedo 8?" Mitscher asks.

Ring doesn't know. No one knows.

21. *Yorktown* Abandoned

Midmorning, before the bombs fell, Admiral Nagumo had ordered the *Soryu* to launch its new high speed reconnaisance aircraft, make contact with the enemy and report back to him on the strength of the U.S. forces. That aircraft is now landing aboard the *Hiryu* after having returned to find its own home carrier a mass of flames. The pilot apologizes to Admiral Yamaguchi because his radio has not been working, but quickly adds that the "enemy has three carriers, not one."

Three! The *Hiryu* doesn't have enough aircraft to fight just one carrier. Yamaguchi passes the information on to Nagumo and Yamamoto, then lives up to his reputation as an aggressive officer by immediately ordering a second strike.

Leading the torpedo-carrying Kates, nine from the *Hiryu* and one lone survivor from the *Akagi,* will be Lieutenant Tomonaga, the early morning Midway strike commander. Tomonaga's left wing tank has a bullet hole in it. When his crew chief mentions the damage, the lieutenant replies, "Don't worry. Leave the left tank as it is, and fill up the other." There isn't time to make repairs. The damaged plane, now consigned to a one-way trip, is moved into position on the *Hiryu*'s flight deck. Several pilots plead with Tomonaga to exchange planes with them. He refuses, silently acknowledging that this will be a suicide

111

mission, probably the first of the Japanese *kamikaze* attacks of the war.

Earlier that morning there had been cheers and cap-waving when Tomonaga lifted off to lead the planes of all four carriers to Midway. Now there is silence. Hands wave farewell. He will not return. Admiral Yamaguchi stands stiffly as the lieutenant's plane becomes airborne at 12:45 P.M.

On the *Akagi* there is complete chaos at this hour. Captain Aoki has ordered the Emperor's gold-framed portrait transferred to a destroyer. It is an indication that he has decided, less than three hours after being attacked, that there is no hope for his ship.

Conditions are much the same on the *Soryu* and the *Kaga*. Violent fiery explosions crowned with oily black smoke can be seen along their sides. They are tortured, writhing derelicts.

In contrast, many miles away, the *Yorktown*'s propellers are turning. The engine room gang has worked a miracle, and the ship has four boilers back on the line. She is moving at 18 knots, putting herself back together and also preparing her dead for burial at sea. From the air the *Yorktown* does not even look like she received three bomb hits. The hole in the flight deck is being covered with pieces of steel fastened over timbers. She cerrtainly won't be as good as new, but she can operate her remaining aircraft without too much trouble. Her fires are out, and she's survived thanks to damage control.

Admiral Spruance has sent over two cruisers and a pair of destroyers, detaching them from his Task Force 16, to help out with antiaircraft fire. Around the *Yorktown* at this moment are twelve ships, each with gun barrels pointing skyward. There is little doubt that there will be another attack on the "Yorky."

The waiting time is short. At 2:26, the cruiser *Astoria* reports that her radar has "bogeys" at 33 miles on a course toward the *Yorktown*. They are flying in level, not climbing, at 7000 feet. Torpedo planes with-

out question. Bells clang as Task Force 17 again buttons up, going to *Zed,* the battle condition.

Circling above the *Yorktown* are six of her own
CAP Wildcats, operating from the *Enterprise,* plus
three more belonging to the "Big E." Soon to join
them are four Wildcats from the *Yorktown,* now being
refueled. But that procedure has been halted by the
air raid alarm. The four fighters, led by Jimmy Thach,
run up engines frantically, preparing to take off with
less than twenty-five gallons in each of their tanks.
They're all prepared to fight and ditch.

At 2:32, Lieutenant Tomonaga orders his planes to
break the approach formation and split up to make
runs on the *Yorktown* from various directions, another
scissors attack. Another two minutes go by before he
orders the strike. The Kates dive for the low altitude
approaches, skimming the water and making antiaircraft fire almost impossible. The escort ships will hit
each other before they will hit the attacking "bogeys."

Jimmy Thach, not burdened by fuel weight, hurls
his fighter into the sky and knocks down a Kate thirty
seconds after his wheels clear the flight deck.

The cruisers, unable to fire at the enemy planes, do
the next best thing—they shoot into the water in advance of the enemy aircraft. Huge geysers rise from
the ocean. But somehow, half the Kates run the gaunt-
let, and four release torpedos.

Captain Buckmaster manages to thread two of the
"tinfish," but the other two slam into the *Yorktown*'s
side, opening up her fuel tanks and jamming her rud-
der. She loses power and is listing seventeen degrees
within a few minutes. Soon she tips to twenty-six degrees and is in danger of capsizing.

Reluctantly Buckmaster orders her to be abandoned
at about 3 P.M., less than thirty minutes after the attack. Her engine room is flooded. The sounds of air
bubbles can be heard as water begins to fill her.

The ships of the escort move in to pick up the *Yorktown*'s crew. The evacuation is orderly. In an hour and
forty minutes, 2,280 men are rescued.

The five surviving pilots of Tomonaga's strike head back for the *Hiryu* without the lieutenant. He did not run out of gas, however. He launched his torpedo, but then his plane disintegrated from machine gun fire, exploding less than a thousand yards from the *Yorktown*.

The returning pilots report to Admiral Yamaguchi that they "hit the carrier, and it stopped." This, then, indicates to Yamaguchi that two of the three American carriers are out of the battle. The surviving pilots of Kobayashi's strike earlier reported knocking one out at noon. But neither Yamaguchi nor the pilots realize that their target has been the same ship both times. They had no way of knowing that the *Yorktown* healed her wounds and got underway again after the first strike. Once again, there is overconfidence and faulty reasoning on the part of the Japanese commanders.

The entire Japanese First Carrier Striking Force is now down to fifteen aircraft all aboard the untouched *Hiryu*. Nonetheless, Yamaguchi plans one final assault against the Americans to sink the remaining carrier and pull victory from defeat.

However, his pilots are hungry and exhausted, having flown missions since dawn. Some have been awake since 1:30 A.M. The admiral decides to postpone the attack until sunset, giving the pilots time to eat and rest. The decision compounds a day of bad decisions by the Japanese admirals. The *Hiryu* is doomed.

22. Four Red Glows

At 4:45 P.M., Lieutenant Earl Gallaher of the *Enterprise* picks up the white wakes of the Japanese task force on the ocean below and signals for his group to climb. They rise to 19,000 feet and circle around to take full advantage of the strong afternoon sun, which will blind the enemy gunners. Gallaher plans to dive out of the path of the sun. Just before pushing over at about 5 o'clock, the lieutenant breaks radio silence to instruct his "Big E" planes to hit the carrier. He assigns Dave Shumway's accompanying *Yorktown* planes to the enemy battleships.

As the dive bombers fall away toward their target, the *Hiryu*'s desperate CAP begins scissoring back and forth across the line of dive bombers with guns barking. Down below the task force finally spots the attackers in the sun's path and begins to maneuver wildly. The *Hiryu* is turned sharply to the right, and Gallaher's bomb falls astern, exploding in the sea. The next five bombs are also near misses, with the *Hiryu* swinging back again, foiling their aim.

Dave Shumway, heading for a battleship, sees the string of bombs miss and turns his *Yorktown* section back toward the carrier. Planes from both the *Enterprise* and *Yorktown* are now diving on the *Hiryu*.

The Zeros have been deadly all day, but this last group above the *Hiryu* are suicidal in their zeal, ripping away with machine gun fire. They are also quite

The Zero

willing to ram the American planes in midair. Half of the Dauntlesses are damaged by enemy gunfire, but three Zeros fall as well.

Finally four 1000-pound bombs reach the target, and half a dozen pilots claim the hits. The first one blows the *Hiryu*'s forward aircraft elevator against the bridge island. The other three explode in the same area, amidships and forward of the island.

The *Hiryu* heaves under the massive blows, but still manages to maintain her thirty knots, though her flight deck is completely destroyed. Within a few seconds, bombs and torpedoes on the hangar deck begin to explode; fire cascades along her length. The few surviving Zeros still aloft will not be able to land on her. They have no place to go but into the ocean.

As the *Enterprise* and *Yorktown* planes haul around and set a course for the "Big E," the *Hornet*'s late-launched flight of sixteen dive bombers arrives and begins a high-explosive treatment of a cruiser and battleship. Then B-17s show up from Midway.

If any of the surviving Japanese admirals need further proof of the American forces will to fight, they get it between the hours of 5:00 and 6:30 P.M. this June 4. The entire sky seems to be filled with Yankee aircraft—Army Flying Fortresses on high, Navy dive bombers down low. At sunset, the American planes mercifully depart. Japan has never suffered such a bitter day at sea.

As darkness begins to settle, the fires of the *Akagi,* the *Kaga,* the *Hiryu* and the *Soryu* cast red glows over the ocean. One officer on a destroyer says that from a long distance, they look like the "traditional lanterns of the homeland." The "lantern" of the *Soryu* is snuffed out at 7:15. She has been drifting since midmorning, a helpless burning hulk, and now she begins to sink. In three minutes she is beneath the surface. Five minutes later, from deep in her grave, there is a tremendous explosion. A giant bubble breaks the debris-littered surface.

The areas immediately surrounding all of the carriers is later described by a Japanese officer as ". . . so terrible that one did not want to look. Oil and dead bodies . . ."

The abandoned *Yorktown* is listing and drifting; a lone destroyer circles her, standing guard against submarine attack. It is an evening of grief mixed with the joy of triumph for the American ships. There are many empty seats in the wardrooms and plane crew messes of the *Enterprise* and the *Hornet*. In terms of lives, victory has been costly. The torpedo squadrons of each carrier are all but wiped out.

On the *Hornet* Captain Mitscher is withdrawn and silent, sitting in his bridge chair with his long-billed baseball cap pulled low over his eyes. As far as he knows, not one member of Torpedo 8 has survived. Thirty men killed. He does not learn of Ensign Gay until later.

23. An Apology to the Emperor

As the *Soryu* begins her death throes, Admiral Yamamoto dispatches a curious message to his anxious and shaken commanders, telling them that the "enemy fleet has been practically destroyed and is retiring eastward." He advises that the Combined Fleet units are "preparing to pursue the enemy, and at the same, occupy Midway." The message is also sent to Tokyo.

By now, Isoroku Yamamoto knows full well that the *Hiryu,* his only hope, has been attacked and is on fire. He also knows that he has little chance of occupying Midway. His message, probably meant simply to bolster morale, is both untruthful and hollow.

Yet he is not giving up. He still seeks night action. The Japanese have always favored night gunnery battles, having trained for them vigorously, and Admiral Kondo's battleships and cruisers, racing now to catch the U.S. forces, are capable of great destruction. The aircraft advantage of the *Hornet* and the *Enterprise* will mean nothing once darkness reaches the Central Pacific. The guns of four battleships and six cruisers can riddle the outnumbered American task force.

It is for this reason that Admiral Spruance has turned the task force eastward and away from the enemy. He is later criticized for not chasing the Japanese throughout the night, but he responds, "I did not feel justified in risking a night encounter with possibly superior forces, but on the other hand I did not want to be too far away from Midway the next morning. I wished to have a position from which to either follow the retreating enemy forces or break up a landing on Midway."

While Spruance is steaming east with his two untouched carriers and their escorts, scheduling a course change back to the west at midnight, Admiral Nagumo, aboard the cruiser *Nagara,* is moving northeastward with his surface ships with all desire for battle completely gone. In fact, he's now considering suicide. He cannot accept the disgrace of defeat.

The early evening message from Yamamoto boldly outlining plans for attack is greeted with despair by Nagumo. "Attack? With what?" The admiral is slowly coming apart as other messages arrive in the *Nagara.* One scout plane message tells him that the Americans have "five carriers," not the three previously reported. Nagumo does not question the scouting report.

But the despair, the inability to think clearly, and the possibility of mental breakdown, is not limited to the *Nagara* bridge. Captain Aoki on the burning *Akagi* orders his staff to leave the ship after they have tied him securely to the anchor deck so that he'll die when the ship sinks. Bound to the deck, he is smiling widely as everyone departs. However, he has a problem—the *Akagi* refuses to sink.

At this same time on the *Kaga,* fire reaches the forward gasoline storage tank, and there are two deafening explosions. The *Kaga* vanishes in the twilight, taking with her hundreds of crew members trapped below. She leaves a pall of black smoke to mark her watery grave.

Now at 9:30 P.M., Admiral Nagumo radios Yamamoto, citing the earlier and faulty seaplane report, "Total enemy strength is five carriers, six heavy cruisers and fifteen destroyers. They are steaming westward." They are, in fact, steaming east.

An hour later, Nagumo sends another message to Yamamoto, "There still exists four enemy carriers. None of our carriers is operational."

The information is maddening and confusing. Five carriers one time, four the next. But what angers Yamamoto most is the despairing tone of the last message. He removes Nagumo from command, assigning him to look after the remains of the burning carriers. It is a devastating comedown for the proud Nagumo.

Yamamoto next orders Admiral Kondo to assume leadership of the remainder of the First Carrier Striking Force, and Kondo immediately plans to utilize the Nagumo surface ships in his "night engagement" with the American fleet. But Kondo also realizes that his best speed will still not permit him to be in position for a night engagement until at least 3 A.M. Then he must search out Spruance before daylight (about 5 A.M.) and close in on him within gunnery range. Once dawn breaks, however, the remaining American planes can give Kondo the same treatment that was administered to Nagumo's carriers. Kondo has no desire for that.

As the clock ticks on, Yamamoto and most of his staff realize that the battle is over. They have lost, suffering the worst military defeat in the history of Japan. No one wants to admit it. There is still brave talk of engaging the enemy, but they are not rational men at this moment.

After heated discussion Captain Kurashima, the planner of Operation MI who was always so inventive in the past, suggests a daylight attack by all their battleships on Midway. Tons of shells will wipe the island out, he says. The shelling will destroy the runway, he maintains.

Chief of Staff Admiral Matome Ugaki turns fiercely on Kurashima, "The stupidity of engaging such shore installations with a surface force ought to be clear to you . . ." Ugaki points out that American aircraft, both land and carrier-based, would sink the battleships before they could get close enough to use their big guns.

Some staff members still cannot accept the defeat, however, and one asks plaintively, "But how can we apologize to the Emperor?" Yamamoto, silent during the various proposals, speaks up at last, "Leave that to me. I am the only one who must apologize to the Emperor."

Midnight is the time for painful decisions by the stocky man who must apologize to the monarch of Japan. At fifteen minutes past the hour, Yamamoto orders Admiral Kondo to abandon the night attack plan and join up with his Main Body.

Spruance had made a wise move after all. Had he not changed course at 7 P.M., he would be facing Kondo's big guns. The danger is eliminated as the Japanese battleships swerve to the west.

Then at twenty minutes past the hour, Admiral Yamamoto orders the Japanese cruisers—now only ninety miles from Midway—to cancel the island bombardment scheduled to begin around 2 A.M.

It is a terrible, nightmarish night for Yamamoto, and it has been a long night for Captain Aoki, too. He's been lashed to the anchor deck of the *Akagi* since darkness set in, hoping the ship would sink. At 12:30 A.M., a boat dispatched from a destroyer reaches the side of the derelict, and Aoki is physically forced into it.

No ship of the Japanese Navy has *ever* been scuttled, purposely sunk. The *Akagi* is dear to Yamamoto, and all evening he's avoided dealing with her. Now, just before 3 A.M., he gives precise orders on how she is to be sunk with torpedoes. It is a moment of great personal grief for him.

Five minutes later he takes the last step—*MI Operation is cancelled*. The fleet will rendezvous for refueling, then head back, some to Japan, some to the big naval base at Truk. Midway is to become a gnawing, bitter memory. It has not become the "Glorious Month of June."

While the operation is being canceled, a junior officer transfers the Emperor's portrait from the *Hiryu* to a destroyer, and Admiral Yamaguchi along with

Captain Kaku descend from the shattered bridge to address the crew. They are about to abandon the drifting hulk. The sea is lit by the moon and the crimson glow from the carrier's fires. After emotional speeches telling the men to fight on and that victory can be achieved, Kaku and Admiral Yamaguchi exchange ceremonial cups of water, then join the men in singing the Japanese national anthem, "Kimigayo."

As soon as the crew and staff members are into the rescue boats, Captain Kaku and Admiral Yamaguchi "admire the moon for a few minutes," then go into their respective, darkened cabins to commit *seppuku* —suicide.

The single Japanese unit in action on this anguished night is the submarine I-168. Under orders to bombard Midway as a prelude to the shelling by the cruisers, Lieutenant Yahachi Tanabe begins firing on the island promptly at 1:30 A.M. Yamamoto's staff has failed to notify him that *Operation MI* is cancelled and the cruisers have been withdrawn. Picked up by searchlights and targeted by American shore batteries, Tanabe wisely descends into the depths.

One more mistake, a serious one, is made at 3:42 A.M. The Japanese cruisers, having turned away from shore, are running northwestward at twenty-eight knots to join the Main Body when the American submarine *Tambor* puts in an unexpected appearance. The *Tambor* reports the presence of the cruisers.

A "red-red," emergency signal for a forty-five-degree turn to port is ordered. All of the speeding Japanese ships receive the message except for the last one in line, the cruiser *Mogami*. When the turn is executed, the *Mogami* smashes the stern of the next cruiser in line, *Mikuma*, crumpling her bow and catching fire. Fuel tanks of the *Mikuma* are ruptured. Yamamoto now has two more casualties, a crippled cruiser and one trailing oil. Both are easy targets for air strikes.

Yamamoto's staff wonders what else could possibly happen. It seems as though a god is wreaking vengeance on the Japanese Navy.

The last Japanese unit near Midway is still the I-168. Spotted by a PBY patrol plane at dawn, Tanabe decides there are much safer waters than those just off the beaches of Sand and Eastern. He slides away into the open ocean in search of an another target. The drifting *U.S.S. Yorktown* is only 150 miles away.

24. Yamamoto Goes Home

At dawn every able PBY on Midway takes to the air again to search for the Japanese fleet. Eastern's diminished air force, having suffered many casualties yesterday, stands by for strike orders. Twelve Army B-17s roll off to go orbiting and await directions.

The night has been short and tiring, mostly spent refueling aircraft by hand. Fueling a B-17 or PBY from fifty-five-gallon drums is similar to filling a reservoir with a thimble. Then there was that futile shelling of the island at 1:30 A.M., which not only interrupted those who were asleep, but also stopped the refueling operations. When that scare ended, the report of enemy cruisers nearby put Midway on alert again. Troop landings usually follow bombardment.

Therefore, the men of Midway are weary and haven't been told that the enemy may be in full retreat and that the danger of an invasion has been greatly reduced. In fact, the end of the day may bring an end to the exhausting alerts.

Now at 6:30 A.M., a PBY reports "two enemy battleships 125 miles away," and Captain Simard immediately orders the orbiting B-17s to the attack. The big bombers hurry off to find the "battleships," which are, of course, the cruisers *Mogami* and *Mikuma*, the former with the smashed bow, the latter trailing oil for miles. They are fine targets, but the Army pilots can't locate them. Simard dispatches his last Marine planes, six Dauntless dive bombers and six of the old creaking Vindicators.

This second wave picks up the oil slick, then follows it right to the stern of the *Mikuma*. No hits are made —except for an unintended sacrifice by Major Richard Fleming. Damaged by heavy antiaircraft fire, Fleming crashes into the after turret of the *Mikuma*. Gas-fed flames spurt out along the deck and are sucked down into the engine room by the vent system. Other fires are started. The *Mikuma* joins the crippled list.

On this morning of June 5, with the weather clear and bright, Admiral Spruance is still exercising caution. The *Tambor*'s sighting of the cruisers off Midway leads Spruance to believe that the battle might not be over. Reports early this morning from a PBY pilot indicate that the *Hiryu* is still afloat. The last time "Big E" pilots saw her, Zeros were in the air. Had they come from the *Hiryu,* or was there still another enemy carrier around? These are among the questions that Spruance ponders this day.

Admiral Nimitz has also been startled by the *Tambor* message, and there has been little sleep in CINCPAC headquarters. The admiral has dozed and cat-napped all night, trying to second-guess Yamamoto's next move.

Hypo intercepts seem to indicate that the enemy is generally withdrawing, yet Nimitz does not trust Yamamoto to do as expected. He issues a warning to Pacific commands, "There are strong indications the Japanese will attempt assault and occupation Midway regardless of past losses." While that message is tapping out from Pearl Harbor to Spruance, Fletcher and the Midway command, Admiral Yamamoto is sorting out his own limited options on the bridge of the *Yamato*.

Few people have ever seen him other than immaculate and clean shaven. In the summer his white uniforms were always crisp and starched. But at breakfast

The Sinking Of The *Mikuma*, June 6, 1942

this day his face is pale and unshaven. His "eyes glitter" as he sits and sips rice gruel Japanese-style, bowl to the lips. His uniform looks crumpled and slept-in.

There is little to encourage him, but he tells a staff member that there is always a chance, if he can lure the Americans into a night surface battle, or if he can lure them to follow his ships closer to Wake Island where land-based bombers can go on the attack.

On the other side, Spruance is looking for Yamamoto and his ships this midafternoon in the American admiral's preferred time of action, the daylight hours. He launches planes from the *Hornet* and the *Enterprise* on a "search and attack" mission. If they find the enemy, they are to attack without further notice.

Before long the weather turns murky, and the pilots have to fly in and out of clouds. The best that fifty-eight planes can do today is flush a lonely enemy destroyer. They bomb it, but claim no hits. The weather has brought low, thickening clouds.

Again there is debate on board the *Enterprise* between Spruance and his staff. Is it at all possible to catch the retreating Japanese fleet?

Obviously Yamamoto's ships are fleeing at best speed except for the two wounded cruisers. Shortly before 9 P.M., Spruance decides he can never overtake the battleships of the Main Body in a stern chase and will have to settle for the cruisers. He turns the task force east again, hoping for a peaceful night.

At daylight on June 6, a reconnaisance flight roars up from the *Enterprise* and soon reports the location of the *Mogami* and the *Mikuma,* moving along at 12 knots and not too far away. A pair of destroyers are chugging alongside to ward off submarine attacks. As soon as morning muster is completed, strike planes roll off the *Hornet,* soon followed by dive bombers from the *Enterprise.*

Not long afterward Admiral Yamamoto receives frantic messages from the *Mogami* and the *Mikuma.*

They report that they're being bombed by carrier-based aircraft. Yamamoto promptly decides to make one last effort to encounter Spruance and the American flattops. At twelve-thirty he orders Admiral Kondo to change course again and run at full speed with his battleships to aid the cruisers. If Spruance stays in the area, Kondo can meet up with him tonight. The admiral then turns his Main Body battleships eastward again and orders additional aircraft flown into Wake Island, hoping that Spruance will stray close enough for medium-range bomber attack.

The *Mogami,* which began this latest cycle of events, somehow survives the bombing and strafing runs of forty-odd aircraft, but the *Mikuma* is sunk with heavy loss of life.

While all this is going on, an effort is being made, at last, to save the *Yorktown.* The big ship is still bravely afloat, and estimates of her early demise are now known to have been false. She is being towed very slowly by a minesweeper. A fleet tug from Pearl Harbor is hurrying out to lend a hand. The chances of her getting back to Hawaii are rather good, barring any other mishaps. Had Captain Buckmaster and Admiral Fletcher been quicker in their efforts to save her, those chances would be much better.

The *Yorktown*'s fire is out, and a salvage team is aboard her. The destroyer *Hammann* is lashed to her starboard side, providing power and pumping capacity. Five destroyers are guarding her, circling her and listening for enemy submarines.

She is still listing badly, but counterflooding will take care of that. The salvage crew is working with cutting-torches to shear off weight—gun tubs and such—from the port side. With luck, she should right herself within twenty-four hours, while awaiting the arrival of the tug. The United States can ill afford to lose her.

Such is the scene when Lieutenant Tanabe of the I-168 shows up at about 1:30 P.M. He sights the badly listing "Yorky" and her screen of five circling destroyers and wastes little time in maneuvering beneath them to fire four torpedoes at a range of 1900 yards.

Two hit the *Yorktown*, and a third crashes into the *U.S.S. Hammann*, sinking her within five minutes. The *Yorktown* is now beyond salvage. Lieutenant Tanabe has fired the last shots of the Battle Off Midway Island.

As the afternoon proceeds, and the Japanese ships hurry back toward the projected position of the American carriers, Admiral Yamamoto does not know that it is Admiral Spruance who has already given up the fight. The objective has been achieved—the invasion of Midway has been stopped and the enemy main carrier strength has been destroyed. The American pilots are exhausted. Many of the aircraft need repair. Fuel in the task forces is running low. There is no further need to remain and protect the *Yorktown*. Admiral Spruance has had quite enough by sundown on June 6.

The next morning Admiral Yamamoto also decides that he's had enough. He cancels plans for any further engagement with the enemy in the vicinity of Midway, reverses the course of his ships once again and sets the Main Body on a heading toward Japan and the Inland Sea anchorage. Enroute to Hashirajima he will keep to himself and say very little to anyone. In time, he will indeed apologize to the Emperor, an act more difficult than facing death itself.

25. Pacific Turning Point

At CINCPAC headquaters on this memorable June 7, when victory at Midway is assured, Admiral Nimitz receives a congratulatory message from the Navy chief in Washington, which is purposely dispatched in plain language so that Admiral Yamamoto and the Naval General Staff in Tokyo can intercept it. In addition to praising the forces that "gallantly and effectively repelled the enemy advance," Fleet Admiral Ernest J. King suggests that the enemy will continue to realize that "war is hell"—a pointed statement for the benefit of Isoroku Yamamoto and his superiors in the Japanese capital.

Later this happy morning Commander Rochefort is invited to an impromptu champagne party at Nimitz headquarters, but he takes so long in shaving and putting on a clean uniform that he misses the festivity. Nonetheless, Nimitz introduces him to other high-level officers as a "man who deserves a major share of the credit for victory at Midway." Typically Rochefort transfers the credit to everyone on duty at Station Hypo in the so-called Black Chamber.

At sea off Midway, ships and aircraft of the U.S. Navy are celebrating, too, but in a different way. They are searching for downed pilots and crewmen—any survivors, American or Japanese. Their efforts have already been rewarded. Ensign Gray of Torpedo 8 has been found. Over the next ten days, twenty-seven airmen are rescued from their rubber rafts.

As one proof of the collapse of organization and the deterioration of morale in the Japanese Navy, the survivors of the cruiser *Mikuma* were abandoned by her escorting destroyers. Some will live to be picked up by American ships and planes.

Midway has often been called the "turning point of the Pacific war," the battle in which Japan lost the momentum and never regained it. Certainly the magnitude of the defeat was such that the Imperial Navy never recovered from it.

Four Japanese carriers were lost between dawn and darkness, and 327 aircraft went down all in the same day. The carriers that were sunk could be replaced, but *not the hundreds of skilled, trained pilots and crewmen.* They were not lost in aerial combat, but rather as sitting ducks on their ships. It is true that most of the Imperial Navy was still intact, but the bitter defeat was a psychological wound that cut deeper than the loss of the submerged hulls of the *Akagi*, the *Kaga*, the *Soryu* and the *Hiryu*. The confidence of—and in—the Imperial Navy had been broken.

The Japanese commanders and high government officials could not accept what had occurred off Midway and silenced the true story, even sealing the lips of such officers as Commander Fuchida, the hero of Pearl Harbor. Newsmen were threatened with imprisonment if they revealed anything other than the official version—a great victory for Japan in the invasion of the Aleutian Islands and a triumph in the Central Pacific. Not until long after the war did the Japanese public learn what had really happened off Midway.

At last, however, the U.S. Navy had something to crow about and did it with big headlines. For security reasons the loss of the *Yorktown* was not immediately acknowledged. Nor was there reason to admit that 147 U.S. planes had been downed. There were positive things to present, like the courage of the pilots from the carriers and Midway Island.

In many respects the Japanese lost the battle in 1940 when JN-25 was broken. The late Professor Samuel Elliott Morison, a naval historian, called the victory "one of intelligence." Task Forces 16 and 17 could not have been waiting in ambush without the work of Stations Hypo, Negat and Belconnen, and the talents of Commanders Rochefort and Layton, and many other unknown radio intercept operators.

Nevertheless, an enormous amount of luck, coupled with mistakes by the Japanese commanders and the arrogance of their "victory fever," contributed heavily to the victory.

From the Japanese there are so many "hads" and "ifs" that speculation over other possible outcomes is not worthwhile. Yet some speculating remains interesting.

Had Admiral Nagumo been thorough and punctual with his dawn searches of June 4, he would have discovered the American carriers, and it is likely that the battle would have been fought differently. It probably would not have been entirely in favor of Spruance and Fletcher.

Had Japanese intelligence been better, the radio deceit in the Solomon Islands waters, placing the *Hornet* and the *Enterprise* deep in the South Pacific, would not have worked.

Had Yamamoto concentrated his ships into one big force, rather than scattering them, the added antiaircraft fire might have made a great difference.

Had Nagumo been decisive about rearming his aircraft after the first report of American ships, he would have gained an hour, making a full strike against the U.S. carriers possible. His planes would not have been caught on deck.

Perhaps the best assessment of credit for the great United States naval victory off Midway is to give one-third to intelligence, one-third to Japanese mistakes and another third to the courageous American pilots.

At the end of the first week of June, 1942, one thing was certain—the Japanese naval war machine was suddenly on the defensive. Midway had stopped its advance—forever. The offensive in the Pacific war now clearly belonged to the United States.

There is an ironic footnote to the Battle Off Midway. That next spring Admiral Isoroku Yamamoto was assassinated in the air over the island of Bougainville in the Solomon chain. Station Hypo intercepted the JN-25 message which announced that Yamamoto would visit Bougainville on a certain day. Rear Admiral Mitscher, former skipper of the *U.S.S. Hornet,* dispatched the P-38s that gunned the Japanese commander in chief out of the sky. Mitscher was thinking of the *Hornet*'s Torpedo 8 that day.

Bibliography

Davis, Burke. *Get Yamamoto.* New York: Random House, 1969.

Dull, Paul S. *The Imperial Japanese Navy, 1941–1945.* Annapolis: Naval Institute Press, 1978.

Forrestel, E. P. *Admiral Raymond Spruance.* Washington: Government Printing Office, 1966.

Frank, Pat and Harrington, Joseph D. *Rendezvous at Midway.* New York: John Day Co., 1967.

Fuchida, Mitsuo and Okumiya, Masatake. *Midway.* Annapolis: Naval Institute Press, 1955.

Johnson, Stanley. *Queen of The Flattops.* New York: E.P. Dutton Co., 1942.

Lord, Walter. *The Incredible Victory.* New York: Harper & Row, 1967.

Lundstrom, John B. *The First South Pacific Campaign.* Annapolis: Naval Institute Press, 1976.

Morison, Samuel E. *History of U.S. Naval Operations in World War II.* vol. IV. Boston: Atlantic, Little Brown & Co. 1962.

Morison, Samuel E. *The Two Ocean War.* Boston: Atlantic Monthly Press, Little Brown. 1963.

Potter, John Deane. *Yamamoto.* New York: Viking Press, 1965.

Sherrod, Robert. *History of Marine Corps Aviation in World War II.* Washington: Combat Forces Press, 1952.

Smith, William Ward. *Midway.* New York: Thomas Y. Crowell, 1966.

Stafford, Edward P. *The Big E.* New York: Random House, 1962.

Taylor, Theodore. *The Magnificent Mitscher.* New York: W. W. Norton, 1954.

Toland, John. *But Not In Shame.* New York: Random House, 1961.

U.S. Strategic Bombing Survey (Pacific), Naval Analysis Division. Washington: Government Printing Office, 1946.

Watts, A. J. and Gordon, B. E. *Imperial Japanese Navy.* New York: Doubleday & Co., 1971.

Index